CW01572687

Best Seller Romance

A chance to read and collect some of the best-loved novels from Mills & Boon—the world's largest publisher of romantic fiction.

Every month, four titles by favourite Mills & Boon authors will be re-published in the *Best Seller Romance* series.

A list of other titles in the *Best Seller Romance* series can be found at the end of this book.

Rachel Lindsay

LOVE IN DISGUISE

MILLS & BOON LIMITED
LONDON · TORONTO

First published 1975
Australian copyright 1982
Philippine copyright 1982
This edition 1982

© Rachel Lindsay 1975

ISBN 0 263 73825 6

Set in Linotype Plantin 10 on 11½pt
02—0382

Made and printed in Great Britain by
Richard Clay (The Chaucer Press) Ltd,
Bungay, Suffolk

CHAPTER ONE

ANTHEA WILMOT took her father's letter into the garden and, settling herself in a deckchair beneath the shade of the chestnut tree, took out the thin airmail sheets covered with the familiar spiky handwriting.

It was unusual for her father to write at such length and she decided that his convalescence must be doing him good. No doubt this letter was full of instructions for the research he wanted her to do prior to his beginning the second volume of his magnum opus—*The Customs of Ancient Britain*. Bending her head, she began to read.

A shaft of sunlight filtering through the leafy bower above her, turned her brown hair to the colour of sherry and gave her creamy skin a golden hue. In profile her face had the serious intensity often found in a child, an impression increased by her high forehead and the rounded curve of her chin.

If anyone had told Anthea she was beautiful she would have burst out laughing, for hankering after the sleek looks of the models whose pictures she admired in *Vogue*, she was not enamoured of her own more voluptuous curves, nor the bouncing vitality which was so much a part of her character. But as she folded the letter and slipped it back into its envelope, some of this vitality faded, tempered by a dismay so profound that it required a great effort not to let it engulf her.

Her father had got married again. Unbelievable but true. A rambling account of the woman who had made him succumb to matrimony was contained within the pages she had just read.

'I know my news will come as a surprise to you,' he had

written, 'but when you meet Maude you will understand why I did it. She is an excellent woman with an unusually good mind.'

Coming from her father this was praise indeed, though she wished he had been less concise in his description. All he had added to this was that, like himself, the unknown Maude had lost her partner several years ago, and that she had been a teacher in a small provincial town.

'Maude is looking forward to university life,' he had concluded, 'and I have assured her she will not be disappointed.'

Wondering what her new stepmother envisaged as university life, Anthea went to break the news to Chrissy, their housekeeper and general factotum ever since she could remember.

'Married!' that good woman said in dismay. 'Why on earth did the Professor do a thing like that?'

'For love, I suppose,' Anthea smiled.

'At sixty?' Chrissy was indignant. 'Really, Miss Anthea, I thought he had more sense!'

Though Anthea privately agreed with the comment it seemed circumspect not to admit it. 'We'd better get the front bedroom ready,' she said.

'Your *mother*'s room?'

'Not any more,' Anthea said gently. 'There's a new Mrs. Wilmot now, Chrissy. We must remember that.'

'Not if it means forgetting the first one.' Tears welled in the faded brown eyes and the housekeeper turned and busied herself at the sink. 'And *you* can't forget so easily either. There's no point telling me you can.'

'Of course I can't forget. I'm merely saying it's wrong for us to go on living in the past. I'm glad my father has remarried.'

'If he was going to get himself a wife, it's a pity he didn't do it before he was taken ill.' Chrissy banged down a pot.

6

'He wouldn't have upset *your* career if he'd had someone else to look after him and help him with his work.'

'Even if he'd had a wife, I would still have left university,' Anthea replied. 'It wasn't much fun for him to be tied to the house for a year; and without me to do his research, he'd never have finished his book.'

An audible sniff was the housekeeper's only comment, and deciding to leave while peace still reigned in the kitchen, Anthea went upstairs.

The front bedroom had not been used since her mother's death ten years ago, though it had been repainted and re-furnished and held no hint of the sadness of its past. She sighed and wondered if her father realised how lucky he was to have had two doting women to care for him all his life. His own mother—whom Anthea remembered as a matriarch in black—then his wife, a woman as spirited and vital as Anthea herself, who had run his home so efficiently that he had been able to devote himself entirely to his work. Her death had temporarily upset the even tenor of his life, but Chrissy had soon managed to cope with all the domestic chores while Anthea had learned to cope with the personal ones.

A year ago this peaceful existence had been broken by his illness. A severe attack of bronchitis developed into pneumonia, and he had been left so debilitated that he had been given a year's leave of absence from university. Anthea had immediately left too—in the middle of her degree course—in order to do the research necessary for her father to continue with his book. She had promised to complete her degree as soon as he was well again, and his trip to Greece this Easter had been the final stage of his convalescence.

Sorting through the linen cupboard, she tried to overcome the fear she felt at the prospect of having to share her home with a stranger. Unworldly though her father was, he would surely not marry someone with whom he was totally

7

incompatible, and this at least meant that she herself would have something in common with the unknown Maude. She took his letter out of her pocket and looked at the last page to check the hour of his arrival. By this time tomorrow he would be home and she would know the worst.

'The best,' she said aloud. 'Think positive, my girl. Think positive!'

Anthea's first sight of her stepmother did little to encourage positive thought. Dressed without concession to the heat or time of day, the new Mrs. Wilmot sailed majestically across the lawn in a tweed suit with complementary hat, gloves and shoes.

'My dear Anthea,' she said in a loud voice, 'I am delighted to meet you. Frederick has told me so much about you.'

Frederick. Hearing her father called this, when for years no one had called him anything other than Fred, a warning bell rang ominously in Anthea's brain. She glanced at her father, but he did not appear to see anything strange in the full use of his name, and was beaming happily at his bride.

'I don't expect you to call me Mother,' the woman went on, 'and you're too old to call me Aunt. I think—yes—I have no objection to you calling me Maude.'

Murmuring that she would be delighted to do so, Anthea wondered where was the charm and intelligence her father had written about. Not until after dinner did some of this emerge, when Mrs. Wilmot settled back in an armchair and urged her husband to talk.

There was nothing Fred Wilmot liked better, and he started by telling them how far he had progressed with his book that day and what his current problems were with it.

Maude Wilmot hung on his every word and, watching her, Anthea had to concede that her interest was genuine. There was no doubt the woman hankered for culture with a capital C, and was overwhelmed at having managed to capture a real live professor. This belief was confirmed by the questions she showered on Anthea, for they showed lively concern with academic life and position.

'It's extremely important for Frederick's students to know they can come here whenever they wish,' she declared emphatically. 'It was a belief my late husband always tried to inculcate in *his* students. But day school doesn't give one the same opportunities. At university it must be quite different. I'm sure the students would enjoy a chance to relax in a homely atmosphere.'

'I have open house once every term,' Fred Wilmot said. 'It's too much work for Chrissy to have it more often.'

'I am sure we can manage to do better than that in future. Wait till you have sampled my cooking, Frederick. When you do you won't be disappointed.' Prominent brown eyes looked at Anthea. 'I suppose you consider cooking a waste of time? Most intellectuals do.'

'Anthea is an excellent cook,' her father interjected mildly. 'You must get her to make you a soufflé; it's one of her specialities.'

'There's nothing difficult about making a soufflé,' Maude Wilmot answered.

'I've arranged the menu for tomorrow,' Anthea said hurriedly. 'But after that, the reins are in *your* hands—er—Maude.'

'Thank you, my dear. I am sure you must be happy to give them up and go your own way again. Your father told me you came back home to look after him when he was ill.'

'I left university,' Anthea corrected, 'but it wasn't a question of returning home. I lived here already.'

'You mean you went to *this* university?'

'I'm reading history. Who better to teach me than Dad?'

Maude made no comment, but her mouth set in an un-

9

compromising line which, in turn, increased the squareness of her chin. Definitely a Maude, Anthea mused with an inward sigh, and in her mind's eye already saw the writing on the wall.

Later that night as she climbed into bed her father came to see her. He had taken off his jacket and she was glad to see he was not so bony. He looked more rested too, though she could not believe this was due to Maude, whom she had found, even on short acquaintance, to be extremely wearing. Not so her father, it seemed, for sitting on the bed, he spoke of his bride with genuine warmth.

'She doesn't make a good first impression, but that's because she is nervous and tries too hard. But she is a sympathetic woman and most capable. I feel I can leave things with her and know they will be done.'

'They always *have* been done,' Anthea said, hurt.

'I know that, my dear,' her father responded. 'Both you and Chrissy have looked after me devotedly. But I don't have the right to command such devotion—certainly not from you. I felt very badly at asking you to give up your own life this past year.'

'I enjoyed it,' Anthea said at once. 'I've learned more working with you than I'd have done if I'd taken ten degree courses!'

'Which brings me back to the reason I came in,' her father replied. 'My marriage must make no difference to you. This is your home and always will be for as long as you need it. There's no reason for you to move into lodgings when you resume your studies.'

Anthea hid her surprise. She hadn't even considered leaving home. To do so was a needless expense and the freedom gained by living in digs in no way compensated for the pleasures of this rambling Victorian house with its lovely garden. Yet her father's remark indicated that Maude had already discussed it with him, and she instinctively knew that the woman wanted her to go. Not that she could blame her for it, Anthea had to admit. If she were in Maude's position she would probably feel the same.

'It might be an idea for me to live out,' she said casually. 'Most girls of my age do.'

'At twenty-one?'

'That's ancient these days!'

Professor Wilmot stood up and kissed the top of his daughter's head. 'Do whatever you wish, my dear. Of course if you move, I will increase your allowance.'

'There's no need for that.'

'You won't find it easy to live on your grant. Anyway, you've been my unpaid assistant for a year. That's worth at least two thousand pounds.'

'Don't be silly. I didn't do it for the money.'

'I know. But I still want to pay you. We'll talk about it another time.'

For a long while after he had gone Anthea considered the future. Maude was right. It would create problems if she went on living here. Chrissy, for one, would not easily accept having another mistress and, if given orders she did not agree with, might well turn to herself for encouragement. Such divided loyalty could only end in discord, and her father would eventually be the one to suffer from it. All things being equal it was advisable for her to find her own place as soon as possible. Provided she did not want anything elaborate it should not be difficult.

Happier in the knowledge that she had made some resolution about her future, she settled herself to sleep, her thoughts turning fleetingly to her own mother, a living memory still, albeit one that could not help her.

CHAPTER TWO

ANTHEA's determination to find somewhere to live received a setback when she discovered the prices being asked for most indifferent accommodation, and though she immediately lowered her standards, the cost of the smallest flat was still far in excess of what she could afford.

Loath to mention it to her father for fear he would see her urgent desire to move as a criticism of his wife, she said nothing at all. So far she was on amicable terms with her stepmother. It meant treading warily, for Maude had her own way of doing things and a deep-seated desire to be the sole woman in charge of the household. But when her father gave a large party to introduce his bride to his friends and the university fraternity, Anthea realised the necessity of getting away while she and her stepmother were still on speaking terms.

When not beset by nervous apprehension Maude was a pleasant if determined woman, but when meeting new people she affected such a gushing manner that she caused uneasiness all round. It highlighted Anthea's own ease and casual acceptance of people with whom she had grown up. After all, it was impossible for her to be in awe of even the most illustrious Fellow when he had dangled her on his knee as a child.

As the evening had progressed, with Anthea being included in all the conversation, Maude's nervousness and irritation had increased, and though she said nothing about it when the party was over, her frustration showed itself several days later.

'It isn't good for you to be around older people all the time,' she exclaimed. 'You should be with your own friends.

You don't even have a young man to take you out.'

'Anthea has plenty of time before concerning herself with boy-friends,' Professor Wilmot said. 'I hope she has the sense to stay single for at least five years. She should see something of the world before she settles down to domesticity.'

'How old-fashioned you are, Frederick,' his wife replied. 'These days marriage doesn't mean domesticity. A married woman can have just as full a life as a single one.'

'Not if she wants to be a good wife and mother.'

'*I* was married when I was twenty,' Maude prickled, 'and I pride myself I was a capable wife without being a dull one. I taught at school with my husband and ran a home.'

'But you are a remarkable person,' Anthea said quickly. 'I don't think I've got the energy and talent to do both jobs well.'

The lightening of Maude's features told Anthea she had lied in a good cause. Like most self-conscious women, Maude responded to flattery no matter how obvious. It was an easy way to curry favour, but Anthea knew she did not have the aptitude to do it for long. Sooner or later temper would get the better of discretion and she and her stepmother would have rows which would·have unhappy repercussions for her father.

'Take the party we gave the other night.' Maude was speaking again. 'There were hardly any young men here and the few that were never got a chance to talk to Anthea because of all the elderly men around her.'

'My friends would resent hearing themselves described as elderly,' Professor Wilmot smiled.

'You know what I mean, Frederick.'

'Yes, my dear, I do.'

The look he gave his wife, followed by the look he immediately gave his daughter, indicated he was not speaking idly, and this only added to Anthea's determination to leave home. The last thing in the world she wanted was to come between her father and Maude. It was obvious the woman had disliked seeing her husband's friends talking to his daughter rather than to herself, and being too insensitive to see this was due to her own behaviour, she had inevitably blamed it on her stepdaughter's desire to outshine her. Without the competition of a younger woman Maude might eventually settle down; it was doubtful if she would ever be completely at her ease, but she must at least be given the chance of finding a niche for herself.

'I've seen several flats,' Anthea murmured casually. 'I'm hoping to find the right one soon.'

'Can't the university help you?' Maude asked.

'I'm hoping they'll do so in October. There's a chance that I can get rooms in college. It's finding somewhere *until* October that's the problem.'

'Aren't the rooms free now?'

'My college is being redecorated,' Anthea replied. 'That's the whole problem.'

'It's not such a problem,' her father intervened. 'After all, you do have a home to live in. No one is pushing you out.'

He did not see the look of annoyance flung at him by his wife, but Anthea did not miss it and was not surprised when, dinner over and Frederick Wilmot retired to his study to glance quietly over some papers, Maude returned to the subject of her moving.

'I don't want you to feel I'm turning you out of your home, my dear. I'm sure you realise yourself that——'

'I do,' Anthea said gently, 'and I agree with you. That's why I want to move. It's the best way for us to remain friends.'

Maude flushed, uneasy at having a spade so plainly called a spade. 'I don't know whether your father gives you an allowance, but I'd never stand in his way if he did,' she continued awkwardly but with determination.

'That's most kind of you.' Anthea turned away to hide an unexpected spurt of anger.

'Mind you,' the older woman went on, 'he's going to have far heavier expenses this year. We'll be doing up the house and refurnishing the drawing-room and dining-room. At the moment I don't feel I belong here.'

'You've only just moved in. It takes time to feel at home.'

'I realise that; but I'll never feel at home unless I feel at ease.' She glanced at the chintz covering on the drawing-room chairs and the faded but still lovely carpet on the floor and Anthea, with very little stretch of the imagination, could envisage the way the room would soon be looking: stiff with formal brocade and flowered Wilton.

She sighed and pushed back the heavy strands of hair that fell across her forehead. It was a graceful gesture, though she was unaware of it. 'I don't need an allowance from my father. He has already been more than generous to me.'

'He's an extremely generous man,' Maude said graciously. 'I'm glad you're not the kind of girl to take advantage of him.'

'I hope you will be the same kind of wife.'

Maude's face went a mottled red. 'Are you being rude to me, Anthea?'

'No more rude than you were being to me. But you like to speak your mind and I'm doing the same. I want you to know I have no intention of being a burden on my father, I'm twenty-one and capable of looking after myself. I would have had my degree already if I hadn't lost a year by leaving university to look after him.'

'You've been a wonderful daughter,' Maude said hastily. 'I'm not trying to push you out, but——'

'*But* is the operative word,' Anthea smiled, her temper

15

evaporating. 'Don't worry, Maude, you'll soon be left in sole charge.'

'You have a strange way of putting things.'

'I see things differently from you.'

'Ah yes, the generation gap!'

Pleased that she had found a satisfactory explanation for the friction, Maude sailed out, leaving Anthea uncertain as to who had won the victory.

Disconsolately she went into the kitchen to fill a thermos flask of coffee. Since her father's marriage she had got into the habit of taking it up with her to her room and remaining there for most of the evening. Maude was right up to a point. She wasn't going out enough. But all the friends she had made at university had now left, degrees achieved, while the ones with whom she had grown up had, for the most part, elected to go to universities in other towns in order to move away from their parents. She had been the only one who had wanted to stay at home, preferring the proximity of her father's company to the ephemeral freedom which living in lodgings would have given her. In this respect her decision had not been wise, and it would be as well to rectify it as soon as she could.

'You look full of dismal thoughts,' Chrissy said, putting away the last of the dishes.

'I'm wondering what job I can get until October.'

'I thought you were helping your father with his book?'

'I've done most of the research necessary. All he needs now is a secretary.'

'Then give yourself a holiday. You deserve one.'

'I don't need a holiday. I need a job. I have to be self-supporting, Chrissy. I can't go on sponging on my father.'

Chrissy opened her mouth to reply, but thought better of it. 'You aren't trained for anything yet,' she muttered.

'Only helping around the house,' Anthea grinned, picking up a tea-cloth to dry some dishes on the draining board.

'That would be one way of getting my board and keep. Do you fancy me as a housekeeper to some dear old man?'

'If I were a dear old man I'd fancy you very much,' Chrissy grunted. 'But you'd be more likely to end up working for some dear old woman who'd have you at her beck and call night and day.'

'I'm sure I could find something fairly decent,' Anthea glanced curiously at Chrissy. 'How have *you* felt about working here all these years? I shouldn't think it's much fun to take care of somebody else's home all your life.'

'It's better than not having a home at all.' Chrissy clattered the cutlery back into the drawer. 'I was never the type to attract a man and I must confess it never worried me very much either. It might have done if I hadn't been happy here, but I've enjoyed every minute of my time with your mother and the Professor. I'm not sure how I feel now,' she said darkly. 'I'll have to wait and see.'

She took off her apron and hung it on a hook on the door. Visible in a brown flowered dress, she looked more homely and older, her brisk efficiency removed with the white overall.

'I'm popping out to see my friend Betsy Evans,' she added. 'I've already taken the Professor his coffee.'

Anthea glanced at her watch. 'It's nine o'clock. Isn't it late for you to go gallivanting?'

'It is—and I'm tired too—but I promised Betsy I'd look in for a chat.'

'Let me drive you,' Anthea volunteered.

'It won't take me long on a bus.'

'It will take you even less by car! Father hasn't put it in the garage yet, so it's no trouble.'

Pleased by the offer, Chrissy accepted. There was not much traffic on the road and they made good time as they skirted the grey stone colleges to reach the council estate that bordered the east side of the town.

'If you can give me an idea how long you'll be,' Anthea said, drawing the car to a stop outside a white-painted gate, 'I'll pop off somewhere for a coffee and come back for you.'

'Why not come in?' Chrissy suggested. 'Betsy would love to see you.'

Anthea smiled and complied. She had known Betsy almost as long as she had known Chrissy, and as a child had enjoyed her visits to this house where she had always been given home-made orangeade and delicious cakes. Betsy had been taking care of her mother then, and selling the vegetables from the large garden at the back of the cottage. But on her mother's death she had taken a job as housekeeper in London. A couple of months ago her employer had died and she had returned to the cottage while looking around for other employment.

Anthea had not seen Betsy for a year and was dismayed by the way she had aged. But she was as agile as ever as she bustled between table and refrigerator, getting out the famous orangeade as she told them of the new post she had just obtained.

'It's with Mr. Allen,' she said, her tone indicating that she expected them to know who he was.

'Is he famous?' Anthea asked.

'He's the financier. I'd have thought you would have heard of him. It's Mark Allen Securities.'

Anthea's brow cleared. She had indeed heard of him. His wizardry with money had reputedly made him one of the wealthiest men in the country.

'It sounds an important job,' Chrissy said. 'Do you think you'll be able to cope?'

'It will be the easiest job I've ever had. More like that of an overseer than a housekeeper. He has a big staff and he employs someone to make sure he always has them! It's my job to see he has no domestic worries. If anyone leaves I have to step in and do their job until I find someone to

18

replace them.'

'The duties of a wife without the pleasures,' Anthea grinned.

'Or the problems,' Betsy chuckled.

'When are you starting with Mr. Allen?' Chrissy asked.

'Next Monday. Not in his London house, though, in his country one near Maidenhead. Bartham Manor it's called.'

'What happened to the woman you're replacing?' Anthea asked.

'She's going to Canada. Her daughter emigrated there a few years ago and is now expecting twins. So Mrs. Goodbody feels obliged to go out and help her. She'd never be leaving Mr. Allen otherwise. She'll be staying another fortnight—to show me all my duties—and then she'll be off.'

'I shouldn't think anyone would need to show you what to do,' Anthea smiled. 'You're as capable as Chrissy.'

'Mr. Allen likes things done in a particular way. When Mrs. Goodbody came to him years ago he made her promise that if she left she'd always train the next housekeeper first. I've had to make the same promise too. The one thing he can't abide is to have his routine upset; everything has to be just so.'

'He's lucky if he can get it,' Anthea replied. 'Still, with all his money I suppose it isn't difficult.'

'He works hard enough to deserve his comforts,' Betsy said, and gave a husky cough and a gasp. 'My chest,' she explained, seeing their startled looks. 'It's been very painful lately.'

'You should have a check-up,' said Chrissy.

'I will once I've settled in at the Manor. But Mrs. Goodbody has been looking for the right person for months and I don't want to let her down. Very particular she was about choosing someone to take her place.'

Driving away from the cottage a little later, Anthea remarked on Betsy's appearance and found that Chrissy had also been disturbed by it. Unaccountably they both felt uneasy, and this feeling persisted even when they reached home.

The ringing of the telephone as they entered the hall made Chrissy pause at the kitchen door as Anthea spoke into the receiver, and it only needed Anthea's frightened look to bring her hurrying forward.

'It's Betsy, isn't it?'

Anthea nodded. 'She collapsed soon after we left. She managed to bang on the dividing wall to attract her neighbour and they called an ambulance.'

'Where has she been taken?'

'The County Hospital. I'll take you there.'

Once again Anthea and Chrissy set off in the car. It was strange that she had chosen tonight of all nights to go with the housekeeper to see her friend. Had she not done so she would not have been involved in this latest drama.

'It's a coronary,' the young house doctor informed them, when they arrived and sought him out. 'Luckily it's a slight one, but she'll have to stay in bed for three weeks and then convalesce for another six.'

'What about her job?' Chrissy asked. 'She's going to a new one on Monday.'

'Not *this* Monday.' The young doctor was positive. 'She shouldn't start work for at least three months.'

'I thought you said it was only a slight attack?' Anthea queried.

'So it is. But the longer she rests, the better. Will *you* be able to inform her employers?'

'Certainly. But we'd like to see Miss Evans if we may.'

The doctor nodded and escorted them to a ward on the first floor. At the far end a bed had been screened off, and here they found Betsy propped up by pillows, a nurse at her side.

'You shouldn't have bothered to come,' she whispered. 'I

feel fine.'

'Don't talk,' the doctor said cheerfully. 'Your friends can only stay a minute.'

'I just wanted to tell you not to worry about your job,' Anthea said quickly. 'I'll telephone Mrs. Goodbody myself and tell her what's happened.'

'She won't be able to wait for me.' Betsy looked unaccountably distressed and Anthea sought for a way of reassuring her.

'I'm sure you'll find another job that's just as good.'

'No, I won't. It's such a beautiful house, and I would have had my own kitchen garden too.'

The thought of Betsy not being able to grow the vegetables she loved so dearly moved Anthea to tears. 'I'll go and see Mrs. Goodbody myself. If I explain that——'

'It won't help. She's booked to go to Canada and she can't change the date. The twins are due in a month.'

'I'm sure she won't leave Mr. Allen in the lurch. You said yourself she promised not to do so.'

'She won't need to leave him in the lurch. There were lots of other applicants. She took *me* because we got on so well together.'

'You mustn't worry about it,' Anthea reiterated. 'I'll go and see her first thing in the morning and come back and let you know the news.'

'It won't be good news.'

'Yes, it will,' Anthea promised, 'because I intend to stand in for you until you're well again.'

Betsy and Chrissy gaped at her and Chrissy recovered her composure first.

'Don't be silly, Miss Anthea. You can't do a thing like that!'

'Why not? I've learned all about housekeeping from you, so I couldn't have had a better teacher!'

'What will your father say?'

21

'He won't know. In any case, why should he object? You know I've been looking for somewhere to live and this will get me out of the house at once. While I'm looking after Mr. Allen I'll have a chance to find a flat. It's an ideal solution. Mrs. Goodbody can tell me all the things she wants Betsy to know and I'll be able to pass them on.'

'Oh dear,' Betsy gulped. 'You're ever so good. I don't know what to say.'

'Say nothing,' Anthea said firmly. 'My mind is made up.'

CHAPTER THREE

BARTHAM MANOR was, in the terms of any estate agent, a gentleman's residence. It was set in rolling countryide, bordered on the west by a river and on its other three sides by arable farms.

Anthea had made an appointment to see Mrs. Goodbody, and parking her car in the wide sweeping drive, was at once overwhelmed by the beauty of the house. It had a charm that came from the elegant proportions of its façade, and this was further enhanced by the beautifully kept flower-beds and sweep of emerald lawn that lay around it like a lush carpet.

Immediately she envisaged Mrs. Goodbody as a black-robed châtelaine carrying a massive bunch of keys at her waist, and knew a momentary trepidation as she rang the bell.

A middle-aged butler opened the door and led her across a panelled hall and through another door into a smaller hall. Here stood the housekeeper. True, there was a bunch of keys at her waist, but in every other respect she was a replica of Betsy Evans.

'You should have come to the staff entrance,' the woman said as she motioned Anthea into a small, well-furnished sitting-room. 'Luckily Mr. Allen is abroad, so no harm has been done.'

Anthea failed to see what harm could have been done if Mr. Allen had not been abroad, but she knew better than to say this.

'Now then, Miss Wilmot,' the woman went on, settling herself in an easy chair and indicating her visitor to do the same. 'What's this about Miss Evans being ill?'

Quickly Anthea explained the situation and offered her own services until Betsy had recovered.

'I could never take you in place of Miss Evans,' came the shocked response. 'You're far too young to have had any experience.'

'I've kept house for my father for several years,' Anthea said firmly, 'and we've always done a great deal of entertaining. He's a Professor at the university.'

'Why do you want a job like this?'

'Because he has recently remarried and I want to move out. I need somewhere to stay until October and if I can work here for the next few months it would be ideal. You can show me everything that has to be done and then I'll be able to show Betsy.'

'It's out of the question. You aren't old enough to take charge of all the servants.'

'Are there so many?' Anthea asked faintly.

'The butler and his wife—she's the cook when Mr. Allen is here on his own, though he brings his French chef from London when he does any special entertaining. Then there's a kitchenmaid, a pantry boy and four other indoor staff, as well as four who work outdoors. I really don't feel you could cope, Miss Wilmot. I appreciate you want to keep the job open for Miss Evans, but——'

'Give me a try,' Anthea pleaded. 'You wouldn't need to

pay me. I'd be happy to accept my board and keep.'

'Mr. Allen would never approve of that. If you come here it would have to be on a proper basis.'

'I'm sure I can manage the staff. After all, it's only a question of getting on with people. And if one can do so with two or three, one can do it with twenty!'

'It isn't as easy as that. Everyone here has their own duties and they guard their responsibilities carefully. You need to be a diplomat sometimes to keep the peace.'

'At least give me a trial for a week,' Anthea reiterated, 'It will take you as long as that to arrange for one of the other housekeepers to come.'

'If any of them are still free,' Mrs. Goodbody replied, and eyed Anthea carefully.

Anticipating that everything would depend on the impression she made, Anthea had chosen the most sober clothes she possessed, and had covered her glossy hair with a hat she had unearthed from Chrissy's cupboard.

'Well,' Mrs. Goodbody sighed, staring at her resignedly, 'if I'm to get to Canada on the day I said, I have no choice but to take you. But it's only until Miss Evans can come here herself. I hope that's clearly understood?'

'Certainly.' Anthea hid her elation. 'When do you want me to start?'

'On Monday—the same as I arranged with Miss Evans.' Mrs. Goodbody stood up. 'Would you like a cup of tea?'

Seeing the offer as a further gesture of acceptance, Anthea nodded and watched as the housekeeper made a pot of China tea and cut several liberal slices from a delicious-looking fruit cake.

'All the food is cooked here,' the woman said as Anthea took a bite and murmured appreciatively. 'Mr. Allen won't have ready-cooked food under any circumstances. The vegetables and dairy produce come from his own farm—and the meat too.'

'Grouse from his own moors, no doubt,' Anthea added.

'Yes indeed. And fish from his own river.'

Hiding a smile, Anthea sipped her tea.

'You will wear black, of course,' the housekeeper continued. 'Never any other colour. A black dress with long sleeves.'

'Long sleeves?'

'It gives you more authority. And being young as well ...'

'Of course,' Anthea said hastily, and made a mental note to go into town that afternoon and buy something suitable.

Being a housekeeper here—even on a temporary basis—would require several additions to her wardrobe. It was money she could ill afford to spend, for she was anxious to save as much as she could while she was here. She sighed. Her father's new life had certainly put a strain on her own.

'Mr. Allen gives his staff a generous allowance for clothes.' Mrs. Goodbody stood up to indicate that the meeting was over. 'But as you will only be here for a couple of months you should be able to manage with two dresses.'

'I don't want to touch the allowance,' said Anthea. 'That belongs to Betsy.'

'I'm sure she won't mind you using some of it. After all, your coming here is keeping the job open for her!'

The housekeeper led Anthea along the servants' hall to a side door. It opened on to a courtyard and through a stone archway she glimpsed part of the main drive.

'Go through the arch and turn right,' Mrs. Goodbody told her. 'It will take you back to the road.'

Demurely Anthea did as she was told, but as soon as the housekeeper had disappeared through the side door she retraced her steps towards the front of the house where she had parked her car. She must learn to behave more circumspectly in future, she thought as she climbed in and drove

25

away. In Mrs. Goodbody's mind, black-garbed house-keepers did not drive scarlet Minis.

That night at dinner Anthea told her father she had found herself a job and would be moving the following Monday.

'A living-in job?' her stepmother exclaimed. 'Who is it for?'

'Mr. Mark Allen.'

'The financier? My dear girl, what an excellent opportunity for you! You're certain to meet a lot of interesting people while you're working for *him*.'

'She meets interesting people here too,' Professor Wilmot said mildly. 'Why does Mr. Allen want to employ a history student?'

It was a question Anthea had foolishly not considered. 'It's more of a—secretarial job than a research one.'

'But you can't type or do shorthand.'

'He doesn't dictate fast and—and there'll be *some* research,' she said hastily. 'It's a book about—about City financiers from the time of Disraeli onwards.'

'I wouldn't have thought Mr. Allen had either the time or the inclination to write a book.'

'He's the sort of man who will make time for anything—providing he wants to do it.'

'Indeed?' said the Professor. 'Tell me more about him.'

Anthea was flummoxed. To admit she had never met her employer would lead to explanations she was unwilling to give, and she racked her brains to try and remember what she knew of the man. Nothing came to mind and she plunged into conjecture.

'He's middle-aged and fussy. Everything has to be just so and—and I think he can be quite tetchy if it isn't. He likes his comforts,' she said, thinking of his beautiful home, 'and he hates having his routine upset,' she added, thinking of the absurdly large staff—both at Bartham Manor and London—who were employed solely to cater to his comforts.

'He doesn't *sound* particularly charming,' her father commented. 'Do you think you will enjoy working for him?'

'I won't be seeing much of him,' Anthea answered truthfully. 'I mean once he's told me what to do, he'll leave me to get on with it.'

'It all sounds splendid to me,' Maude Wilmot commented and, delighted at the prospect of having the house to herself at last, relaxed in a way she had never done before.

It made Anthea more glad than ever that she was leaving. Her father and stepmother needed to be alone together without her own presence to cause friction.

That night, as she sorted through her clothes and books, she was not unduly surprised when her father came in.

'About this job with Mr. Allen,' he began purposefully, 'I hope you aren't taking it because of Maude? As I said before, this is your home and you are always to regard it as such.'

Anthea jumped up from the floor where she was packing her clothes into a case, and hugged him. 'It's sweet of you to say so, Dad, but my staying here wouldn't work. When Maude and I aren't living together, we'll get on much better.'

'I'm sorry you don't like her.'

'I do like her,' Anthea said quickly. 'She's the right sort of wife for you, and that's more important than anything else.'

'I suppose my friends regard her as an unexpected choice too,' Professor Wilmot sighed. 'But she is sensible and down to earth and she knows exactly how to take care of me.' He sighed. 'It wouldn't have been fair of me to have continued relying on *you*. And as long as I remained a widower you would have worried about me and not had a life of your own.'

'You didn't have to marry for *that*.'

'It seemed a sensible reason.' He smiled slightly, his thin face with its untidy grey locks, looking puckish. 'Maude is quite different from your mother, as I'm sure you are aware, and that's sensible too. It's never good to compare one person with another.'

'I know you'll be happy,' Anthea said. 'And I'm doing the right thing by going away. I won't be all that far, you know.'

'That's true; and from October I'll be seeing you at your tutorials. Will your research for Mr. Allen be over by then?'

'Definitely. So I hope you'll use your influence to get me decent rooms in college?'

'What's a father for?' he chuckled, and went out looking more relieved than when he had come in.

On Monday morning Anthea presented herself at Bartham Manor. She was suitably clothed for the part in a black wool dress two sizes too large, thick black stockings and flat-heeled lace-up shoes. Steel-rimmed glasses with plain lenses—which she had once worn in a school play—masked her large grey-green eyes, and unflattering beige powder veiled her creamy skin. Lipstick in an unbecoming shade of purple hid the lovely curves of her mouth and her glossy chestnut hair was pulled away from her face and plaited round her head. The style added several years to her appearance and as she followed the butler down the servants' corridor to Mrs. Goodbody's room, she was reminded of Jane Eyre and hoped there would be no Mr. Rochester in her own life.

With surprising ease Anthea settled into her new position. All the staff had been at the Manor for many years and needed no supervision to ensure they did their work.

She was at a loss to understand why Mr. Allen needed to employ a housekeeper here, for Mrs. Leggat, the cook, could quite easily have done what was required.

It was only as the days passed and she learned more about her duties that she realised she had misjudged the position. Her employer, it seemed, did not so much require a housekeeper as a stand-in-wife. Whenever he was in residence it was her duty to see that there were fresh flowers in his bedroom and library each day; that the humidors were filled with cigars—which she had to finger-test for freshness—and that a stack of new magazines and daily papers were always kept in the drawing-room where the pillows were never to be allowed to stand stiffly against the backs of the settees, but had to be carefully disarrayed to give the room a lived-in appearance.

'Mr. Allen can't abide the place looking as though the decorators have just stepped out,' Mrs. Goodbody explained. 'I've known him come in and sit in every chair just to squash the cushions!'

Anthea's image of the financier began to be somewhat distorted. 'But you say he likes things to be tidy?'

'Tidy but homely.'

'He sounds an awful fusspot,' Anthea muttered, and immediately regretted the comment as she saw Mrs. Goodbody frown. 'I'm just worried in case I do anything to upset him,' she added hastily.

'He'll let you know if you do! He can be sharp when he sees fit. But he's always fair.'

'Is he a widower?'

Mrs. Goodbody pursed her lips and considered the question. Then deciding it was a justified one, she answered it.

'He was engaged years ago, but it was broken off. Ever since then he's felt that women are more interested in his money than in him.'

Anthea sniffed irritably. 'Why do rich men always think

they're being married for their money?'

'Perhaps because they usually are!'

'Then they've only themselves to blame. Most of them have nothing else to offer a woman except a bank account.'

'Mr. Allen has a great deal to offer besides money. He's a most cultured and intelligent gentleman.'

Privately Anthea did not agree. Apart from the antique furniture and English landscape paintings on the walls—which all looked as if they had been bought with the house—there was no sign of Mr. Allen's culture *or* intelligence. She had not even seen a book except for the library, where yards of leather-bound volumes in pristine condition lined the walls.

However, later that week when she was shown into his bedroom for the first time, she was obliged to revise her opinion. Here she found shelves crammed with well-thumbed books on travel, history and philosophy. There were no novels and, surprisingly, nothing on finance. But perhaps Mr. Allen felt he already knew everything about that subject!

It was strange to learn about a man via his possessions, and each one added another piece to the jigsaw of his personality. But there were still many gaps missing. From the expensive stereo equipment—both in the library and bedroom—she knew he was fond of music, but his taste here was as austere as she had expected, with a disproportionate amount of Bach and Purcell, the latter being one of her pet aversions. Clothes—which would have given away much more of his personality—were kept in locked wall cupboards, and opened only by Mr. Allen or his valet.

'We only take care of the clothes if Mr. Allen is away for a long time,' the housekeeper explained. 'And then it's just a matter of airing them. Otherwise it's more than my life is worth to touch anything. He can't abide a cufflink out of place.'

'I bet he's never lost one!'

'Indeed no.' The woman looked shocked at the thought. 'But when he's down here by himself he mostly wears woollies.'

Anthea at once pictured him in faded cashmere with a scarf around his neck. More and more he was beginning to take on the image of Scrooge. His attitude to money was different, of course, but he certainly possessed the same irascible temperament.

'He sounds so difficult that I'm surprised you've stayed with him,' she commented one evening towards the end of the week as she enjoyed a cup of tea with the house-keeper.

'You'll never find a nicer man to work for,' came the instant reply. 'I wouldn't be leaving now if it weren't for my daughter begging me to go and live with her. Providing you follow the rules he lays down and don't bother him with a lot of gossiping nonsense about the servants, he'll leave you completely alone.'

Since this was exactly what Anthea wanted, she made a vow to follow his rules come what may.

'Where is Mr. Allen now?' she asked.

'In Hong Kong. But he should be back any day. His secretary always telephones to let us know when he's due. He spends most weekends down here when he's in England, and in the summer he'll come once or twice during the week too. It depends how busy he is.'

'Does he do much entertaining?'

'More in London than he does here. But if he gives a house-party he always brings Monsieur Marcel, the chef. You must watch out for *him*,' Mrs. Goodbody sniffed. 'He's French.'

Anthea was not sure what this was meant to imply, but considered it would be wiser to wait and see. Looking at her reflection in the mirror in her room later that night, she concluded that she would not need to fear any man—French or otherwise.

She had become so accustomed to seeing herself swathed from head to mid-calf in black that it was a pleasure to undress and see her creamy arms and legs. It was a good thing she was not going to be here in the summer, for nothing would have induced her to go around looking like a mourner at a wake when the sun was shining. How typical of Mr. Allen to insist on his housekeeper wearing such a miserable uniform! He seemed a typical old bachelor. It was a pity he hadn't married. A wife might have made him less of a curmudgeon. She tried to envisage the sort of woman who might have married him, but she could only conjure up a picture of Maude. Hastily she put the thought aside, for Maude was her reason for being here.

Yet in an odd sort of way Anthea was enjoying her charade and daily drew more proficient at playing it. Only at night, alone in her room, did she relax from her role and settle in bed with one or other of the books she had borrowed from Mr. Allen's room. They all bore his name on the fly-leaf; a firm signature with a curving "A" and well looped "l's", unlike the narrow, rigid man she considered him to be.

On Saturday she went home for the day. Mrs. Goodbody was flying to Canada the following weekend and she suggested Anthea might like to have a complete break before commencing her duties.

'It's pointless for us both to be here twiddling our thumbs, and I'm sure you'd like to go and see Miss Evans as well as your parents.'

'I certainly would,' Anthea said warmly, and was so delighted at the prospect of a weekend away, with the chance of putting on her own clothes, that she almost hugged the plump little woman.

Her week's absence from home had further increased her stepmother's friendliness and she greeted Anthea like a long-lost daughter, bombarding her with questions about her work and her employer.

Unwilling to fabricate any more lies about him or the research work she was supposed to be doing, Anthea said he had gone abroad and that she had spent the week procuring the reference books he had asked her to get for him.

'If he's still away next weekend, you must come over again,' Maude said.

'I don't see what his being away has to do with it,' Professor Wilmot intervened, glancing at his daughter. 'You don't work a seven-day week, do you?'

'Of course not,' Anthea said hastily. 'But Mr. Allen likes to work whenever the mood takes him. And weekends are his best times.'

To forestall further questioning she complimented her stepmother on the lunch: a delicious home-made paté followed by a creamy chicken and mushroom pie and crisply cooked vegetables.

'Maude is an excellent cook,' her father beamed. 'I told you she was.'

'I'd substitute the word fabulous,' Anthea enthused.

'I enjoy cooking,' Maude confessed, 'especially cakes and pastries. If you give me warning next time you're coming home, I'll make you a gâteau St. Honoré. It's a speciality of mine.'

Deciding that in every person there was a talent waiting to bloom, Anthea went to see Betsy Evans in hospital.

She was making good progress and was delighted to know her job was safe for her. 'At least there's no chance of you wanting to make it a permanent takeover,' she twinkled.

'No indeed,' Anthea grinned. 'But it's come at just the right time for me.'

33

'Every cloud has a silver lining.'

'I'm sure your cloud has gone for good,' Anthea gave the bony shoulder a gentle squeeze. 'You're looking heaps better after your rest.'

'I think my last job *was* a bit strenuous,' Betsy admitted.

'You'll find your new one a piece of cake. Honestly, it's money for jam! The house practically runs itself.'

'Emergencies always come when you least expect them,' Betsy replied, and Anthea hid a smile at the gloomy tone.

'Well, *I'm* helping you to cope with this particular emergency,' she said breezily, 'and once you're at Bartham Manor your worries will be over.'

'I can't thank you for what you're doing for me.'

'It's my pleasure. It's given me a place to stay until I can find a flat.'

This knowledge was with her when she returned to the Manor late on Sunday afternoon. The front of the house was already in shadow, but as she walked round the side to the servants' entrance—she had learned her lesson and never used the main door—she was unexpectedly warmed by the last rays of the sunset.

She stopped and raised her head to the sky, experiencing a sudden rush of pleasure as she felt the warmth on her face. Though her skin was masked by beige powder it had a glow about it, and the man coming out of the large four-car garage paused to stare at her with a look of mingled surprise and pleasure. With her old-fashioned clothes and unstylish plait, she looked as if she had stepped out of an ancient woodcut.

Hearing footsteps, Anthea turned and saw a tall, dark-haired man watching her. He wore black slacks and a sweater which in no way relieved his taciturn air. Heavy-rimmed glasses added a further look of severity to his appearance as well as masked his expression, though his

34

thin mouth and clenched jaw was indicative of either tension or bad temper. But when he spoke his voice was mild, and she wondered if his air of strain was an integral part of his character.

'Are you looking for someone?' he asked.

'I'm on my way to the house. I work here.'

Narrow dark brows rose. 'As what?'

'The housekeeper. At least I will be once Mrs. Goodbody leaves.'

'You!' This time his surprise was evident. 'Mrs. Goodbody said she'd engaged a middle-aged woman. You can't be more than thirty-five.'

She hid her delight that her disguise was so successful. 'I don't see that my age is any business of yours.'

'Mrs. Goodbody must be mad!' He spoke as if he had not heard Anthea's comment. The mildness had gone from his voice and it was as astringent as antiseptic. 'What happened to the other person she engaged?'

'Miss Evans was taken ill and I'm standing in for her. She should be well enough to start in three months.'

'The whole thing's crazy!' He ran a hand through his hair, ruffling the top of it.

It made him look younger and she guessed him to be in his early thirties; the thirty-five he had assumed *her* to be. He stooped to pick up the wash leather he had dropped at his feet and continued to stare at her in an exasperated fashion.

'Mrs. Goodbody had no business taking you. She should have engaged someone else.'

'I don't see why. I'm perfectly capable of managing this house, and before I leave I'll show Miss Evans exactly what she has to do.' Annoyed that she was explaining herself, Anthea added: 'I still don't see that it's any business of yours.'

'I like to know what's going on.'

'How would you like it if I told you how to keep your cars clean?'

'I beg your pardon?'

'Well, you wouldn't, would you?' she persisted. 'So I suggest you look after your job and leave me to look after mine.'

'I at least know how a car works,' he said sharply.

'And I know how to manage a house!'

'Where did you work before you came here?' he demanded.

'I took care of my father.'

His look of astonishment surprised her until she remembered she was supposed to be thirty-five, and she lowered her head to hide a smile. 'He liked to have me stay at home,' she murmured. 'He's very old-fashioned.' She felt his eyes on her ancient black dress and coat—a bargain she had picked up in a jumble sale yesterday afternoon— and again she bit back a smile. 'It was quite a large house, you see.'

'Large enough to equip you with the knowledge of how to run this one?'

'This place practically runs itself,' she said airily. 'After all, if a pack of servants can't manage to look after one old man, then——'

'He's not so old!' the chauffeur interrupted, and Anthea coloured. What was she thinking of to gossip to this man about their employer?

'You talk as if you know him well,' he went on.

'You know I don't,' she retorted. 'Though when you've done nothing for a fortnight except learn about one man's eccentricities, you feel as if you've known him for years!'

'I don't consider him eccentric,' the chauffeur said.

'Perhaps you've been with him too long to notice any more.'

He pushed his lower lip forward. It was a full and sensual one. 'Why do you call him eccentric?'

Her shoulders straightened. 'I have no wish to gossip with you about Mr. Allen.'

'A highly commendable trait. I hope you'll go on maintaining it.'

'Mrs. Goodbody has already informed me that reporters often come here prying.' Her eyes narrowed, accentuating their sloe shape. 'You aren't a reporter pretending to be a chauffeur, are you?'

For the first time he smiled, showing even white teeth that made her aware of his bronze skin. Even with his black-rimmed glasses he was extremely good-looking, with a sharp, masculine virility that made her notice his height and the unexpected breadth of his shoulders.

'Well?' she said sharply. 'You haven't answered me.'

'I'm not a reporter. You don't need to worry about that.'

With a shrug she moved towards the side entrance. He did not follow her, but as she unlocked the door she glanced over her shoulder and saw him watching her.

Upstairs in her room, unpacking her weekend case, she wondered whether he came down from London every time Mr. Allen did. It seemed logical to assume he did, though if Mr. Allen spent several days in the country he might not want his chauffeur lounging around doing nothing. The thought made her smile. The house was big enough for a regiment to be usefully employed here.

Tweaking her skirt into position, she went in search of Mrs. Goodbody, whom she found sipping the inevitable cup of tea in her sitting-room.

'I didn't expect you back until later,' she smiled. 'But I'm glad you're here. I've got used to your company.'

Anthea acknowledged the compliment with a modest nod. 'I see Mr. Allen is home. When did he arrive?'

'Early this afternoon—and without any warning. It's

37

most unlike him to do a thing like that. But apparently he finished his trip a day earlier than he had expected and flew home without telling anyone. He didn't even telephone from the airport, just drove up without a word.'

'Perhaps he wanted to catch you out eating his caviar and using the best silver!'

In shocked tones Mrs. Goodbody asserted that her employer would never stoop to snooping. 'That's one reason he's so particular about the people he employs,' she concluded. 'Once you have his trust, you're left to get on with the job.'

This didn't go with the fussiness with which Anthea had invested him, but she decided it was wiser to change the subject.

'Does the chauffeur always come down with him?'

'Sometimes Mr. Allen likes to drive himself. He says it relaxes him. But you don't have to worry about Mr. Herbert. He has his quarters above the garage and he rarely comes to the house. If he's here for any length of time his wife comes from London with him.'

Anthea was dismayed at her disappointment. 'I didn't know he was married.'

'Has been for five years. Very pretty she is, too.' Mrs. Goodbody glanced at the clock on the mantelshelf. 'Which reminds me, I want to introduce you to Mr. Allen. He'll be going up to London first thing in the morning and I'll have left by the time he comes down next weekend.'

The thought of being in sole charge of the Manor suddenly assumed gigantic proportions, and Anthea wondered what she had let herself in for. But to think this way was playing into Mr. Herbert's hands. She pulled a face. What an unromantic name for such a good-looking man!

'Come along,' said Mrs. Goodbody. 'I'll take you to Mr. Allen before dinner. He's usually in a good mood then.'

'Wouldn't he be in a better one *after* he's eaten?'

'He likes to listen to music afterwards and he hates being disturbed.'

'Bach and Purcell,' Anthea murmured as she followed the housekeeper into the hall.

'Lots more besides that. He has hundreds of tapes in the library. The one thing you must never do is to interrupt him when he's listening to them. He really does get cross then.'

'I'll make a note of it.'

Anthea took a small diary from her pocket and scribbled in it. Here she had jotted down all her employer's foibles, and intended to type them out for Miss Evans, together with any additional peculiarities which she discovered for herself. It seemed she was learning more new ones about him every day. Yet Mrs. Goodbody seemed fond of him and spoke of him in an almost maternal way. Perhaps elderly bachelors brought out the mother in her. She looked up and saw that the woman was already opening the library door.

'I'd like to introduce Miss Wilmot to you, sir. She'll be running the house for you until Miss Evans is able to take over.'

Bending to replace a smouldering log on the fire, the tall man in a maroon velvet smoking jacket straightened and, poker in hand, swivelled round to regard Anthea. The light of a standard lamp sharpened the planes of his face, highlighting the shadows beneath the cheekbones and making the eyes behind the glinting lenses even more inscrutable.

'Good evening,' he said in a mild voice, and then looked at Mrs. Goodbody. 'You can leave us, thank you. I'd like to talk to Miss Wilmot alone.'

The housekeeper withdrew and Anthea clasped her hands together and waited.

'Don't look so apprehensive, Miss Wilmot,' he said in a tone as dry as the Sahara. 'I don't make a habit of shooting clay pigeons!'

'That's very kind of you,' she said aloofly, and then added hurriedly: 'Sir.'

He put down the poker and rubbed his fingers on his handkerchief. 'Mind you, I don't usually get mistaken for my chauffeur.'

'You wanted me to think you were,' she said before she could stop herself.

'On the contrary, Miss Wilmot. You assumed it without any need for me to pretend. Mind you, it was an understandable mistake.'

'And you let me go on thinking it.'

'It had its amusing side.'

'Mrs. Goodbody said you never snooped.'

'I beg your pardon?' He was no longer amused and she felt her heart beat faster.

'Well, that's what it seemed to me,' she said defensively.

'I can assure you I wasn't. I have neither the time nor the inclination to—er—snoop, as you call it.'

She knew he was speaking the truth, but her irritation remained, caused more by the knowledge that *she* had made a fool of herself rather than of *his* having done so.

'Actually,' he went on, 'I'm curious to know why you assumed I would be in my dotage. Surely my business reputation alone doesn't warrant that description? You do know who I am, of course?'

'Of course. But your habits—the way you like things done—made me think you were old—I mean elderly.' She saw his mouth tighten and said quickly: 'I know very little about people in the City. I don't make a habit of reading the financial news.'

'I'm glad to hear it,' he said crisply. 'Stick to housekeeping, Miss Wilmot. It suits women better.'

Her cheeks flamed and she bit back a sharp retort. 'Did you wish to talk to me about anything in particular, sir?'

'No. When we met this afternoon you told me as much as

I needed to know.'

'Then may I go?'

'By all means.'

Her hand was on the door when he called her back. 'If I find you unsatisfactory, Miss Wilmot, I won't keep you; good deed or no good deed for Miss Evans.'

'I don't expect you to be charitable, sir, merely fair.'

'I always try to be fair.' He bent to the fire again, and knowing herself dismissed, she went out.

In the hall she paused; her pulse was racing as if she had run up a flight of stairs and the bodice of her dress was sticking to her skin. What bad luck that she had met Mr. Allen this afternoon! It had put her on the defensive and from now on she would have to be doubly careful not to arouse his ire. It would be a pity if—after having gone to all the trouble of getting this job—she wouldn't be able to keep it for Betsy. The thought was sobering and remained with her for the rest of the evening, helping to lessen the antagonism she felt towards the man who sat alone in his library absorbed in a world of music.

CHAPTER FOUR

MRS. GOODBODY departed for Canada the following Friday and at last Anthea felt she was going to be put to the test.

Even without the presence of its owner, Bartham Manor was an onerous responsibility, for it was a veritable treasure house of antique furniture and paintings, and as such, was a burglar's paradise. Luckily there was an elaborate alarm system linked to the local police station, as well as three Alsatians who roamed the grounds and were cared for by one of the gardeners. But she made it her business to acquaint herself with the dogs, one of whom attached itself

41

to her side whenever she went for a walk.

Having made her employer's acquaintance—she could not in all honesty put it higher than that—she found herself seeing the house more as a home and less as a setting for an unknown tycoon. But she still could not place him in his background and wondered how he had acquired all the objets d'art he owned. Had he handed someone a blank cheque and given them orders to buy the best, or had he himself gone the rounds of the sales rooms and elegant antique shops?

She half hoped he would not come down to the country the first weekend she was on her own, but he arrived very late on Friday evening, his secretary having called to tell her he would not be requiring dinner. Nervously Anthea went through the main rooms to make sure there were fresh flowers everywhere and left a thermos of coffee and some sandwiches in his bedroom in case he fancied a snack.

It was not until Saturday morning—when she was coming out of the drawing-room carrying some old magazines—that she finally saw him. He was as casually dressed as he had been the first time they had met, and wore slacks and sweater almost the same cinnamon shade as her own hair. It made him look less sombre, though he was unsmiling as their eyes met. It was difficult to see their colour behind his dark-rimmed glasses and she would have liked to have seen him without them.

'Well,' he said crisply. 'Nervous of being left in sole charge?'

'Not at all, sir.' She pulled down the cuffs of her dress and stood primly before him, waiting for him to speak. But he did not do so and with a slight inclination of his head he walked past her.

They did not meet again for the rest of the day, though she was aware of him about the house. He ate lunch in solitary state in the huge dining-room and afterwards went for a long walk in the grounds, returning shortly before dinner which he took on a tray in the library. She was not sure if he watched television, worked or listened to music, but when she went out for a breath of fresh air before going to bed she glimpsed a chink of light through his curtained windows and was curious to know why he chose to spend his time alone; a man in his position must surely have a host of friends.

On Sunday the same pattern was repeated, and Anthea was surprised he was not bored by it. For her own part, she had plenty of time on her hands too. The servants had been in their jobs so long that they knew exactly what to do, and apart from a brief chat with them each morning, she kept her supervision minimal. Her daily inspection of the house did not take more than half an hour and so far she had not found anything to complain of. If she did, she hoped she would have the courage to verbalise it.

On Sunday evening she got down to her own private studies. Her year's absence from university had left her rusty regarding the two previous years' work she had done, and she had set herself the task of re-reading a great many of her books. It was harder than she had expected to re-immerse herself in her curriculum, and not for the first time she doubted her wisdom in having chosen to read history. Naturally it had pleased her father, but she was not sure if it still pleased *her*. But it was too late to change her course now, besides being a waste of all the work she had done to date. She would wait until she obtained her degree and then see if she still felt disinclined to teach or to do research.

Making a face at the heavy tome in front of her on the table, she pulled it forward, and was soon absorbed in Europe in the sixteenth century, so intrigued by the fight for power between the various cardinals of Spain and France that she did not realise she was being watched until the scraping of a chair made her look up.

Mr. Allen had come into her sitting-room and was leaning against the side of a winged chair. In a deep blue velvet smoking jacket, and with his tanned skin and black hair, he looked like a figure in an Ingres portrait. Again she felt curious about his background and wondered if he was as aristocratic as he appeared. Hastily she went to stand, but he waved her to remain where she was.

'Don't disturb yourself, Miss Wilmot. I merely came in because I'll be leaving early in the morning and I wanted to let you know I'm having a house-party next weekend. Two couples, possibly three.'

'Very good, sir. I'll see everything is made ready.'

'One of the couples will be Jasper Goderick and his wife. Please see that Mr. Goderick has the South Suite and his wife the one next to it. And ring my secretary on Tuesday to check if any of the guests have any special preferences as to food.'

'I'll check in my own book first,' Anthea replied. 'If your guests have been here before, Mrs. Goodbody will have made a note of their likes and dislikes.'

'Ah yes, I hadn't thought of that. Good.'

His eyes lowered to the table and the pile of books on it. He did not pick any of them up, but she saw him stare at a couple of the titles before he crossed to the door and went out.

With a snap Anthea closed the book she had been reading. She would not be able to concentrate on it any more tonight; her employer's entry had destroyed her peace of mind.

Pushing back her chair, she went over and unlocked the bureau that stood in stolid mahogany splendour next to the window. Inside she found the book she wanted; leather-bound with thick pages faintly ruled in blue, and half of them already filled with the names and dates of the house-parties given at Bartham Manor. An index in the front alphabetically listed the names of all the guests, and the Godericks, she saw, were among the most frequent visitors.

Mr. Goderick had an aversion to cooked cheese and was not partial to fish. He smoked heavily and Mrs. Goodbody had made a note that the ashtrays in his room had to be doubled. His wife on the other hand was a non-smoker; she liked her bed-linen changed every day and one of the housemaids was always assigned to her during her stay to take care of her clothes which, again according to the book, required a great deal of skilled attention.

Anthea wished she had had the sense to go through this book with Mrs. Goodbody herself, but it was too late now. She could only pray that the information in it was up to date and correct. It would be embarrassing—to say the least—if anything went wrong with the first house-party over which she would be in charge.

Replacing the book in the bureau, she went into the kitchen to make herself a cup of chocolate. One of the maids had suggested bringing it to her each night, but she had refused, preferring to potter alone in the beautifully equipped kitchen, with the opportunity to look at the well-stocked larders and the two huge deep-freeze cabinets purring in the corner.

She was in the act of filling her cup when Mr. Herbert came in: the real chauffeur, as she now thought of him. Small and neat, his face was as shining as the polished buttons on his grey uniform jacket. It was unusual to see him in the kitchen, for he normally remained in his quarters above the garage.

'Is anything wrong, Mr. Herbert?'

'I need a clock, Miss Wilmot. My alarm has broken.'

'Won't the operator give you an alarm call?'

'My phone is only connected to the house, not the exchange.'

'Of course,' she apologised. 'If you let me know what time you want to be woken up, I'll have someone call you in the morning.'

'We'll be up and away long before any of you are stirring! Mr. Allen has an early meeting in the City so we'll be leaving here by six-thirty.'

'In that case you'd better take the kitchen clock.' Anthea handed it to him. 'Don't forget to give it back to me in the morning. *I*'ll be seeing you before you leave,' she added as he was about to interrupt. 'I'll make Mr Allen's breakfast myself. Cook and her husband are staying in the village tonight. It was her sister's twentieth wedding anniversary and they went off this afternoon.'

'You should have told Mr. Allen. I'm sure he wouldn't want you to disturb yourself.'

'Why not? It's my job.'

The chauffeur smiled briefly, thanked her again for the alarm clock, and departed.

Afraid of oversleeping, Anthea only dozed fitfully, and was awake and dressed long before her own alarm rang out. It was still dark so early in the morning, and the stars had not yet faded in the sky, though the birds were beginning to stir as she sped down the servants' stairs to the kitchen.

The house was as warm as it always was. The thermostatic heating kept it at an even temperature and there was no shivering discomfort to overcome as she squeezed fresh oranges for juice and laid the silver tray with Mr. Allen's breakfast china, embroidered napkin and ivory-handled knives and spoons. The marmalade was in a silver container and the eggcups were silver too.

She glanced at her watch. Six o'clock. Speeding down the servants' corridor, she opened the door to the main hall. The house was silent, but even as she listened she heard a light tread on the carpet stair. Hurrying back to the kitchen, she set the eggs to boil, and four minutes later carried the heavy silver tray into the breakfast-room.

Her employer was standing by the window looking out at the slowly lightening garden, the green grass still dipped with dew.

'Good morning, Miss Wilmot.' There was barely perceptible surprise in his voice. 'Where is Leggat?'

'He and his wife stayed in the village last night. They had a family party.'

'You made my breakfast?'

'Yes, sir,' she said without expression, and set the tray on the table. 'I didn't know if you wished to have something more substantial so early in the morning.'

'Eggs will be fine, thank you. But if you'd told me about the Leggats last night I would have told you not to bother with my breakfast. When I leave so early I usually just have coffee.'

'I would still have had to make it, sir, and once I'm up there's no reason why you can't have a proper breakfast.'

Unexpectedly he chuckled. 'I love the phrase "proper breakfast". It makes you sound like my old nanny.'

'I feel it,' she said without thinking.

'Indeed?'

Though the word itself was a question, his tone implied disinterest, which was just as well since she would have been hard put to explain why she felt like his nanny. Flinging a look of dislike at her black-covered arms, she vowed that the minute his car disappeared down the drive she would put on something less conducive to depression.

'Will that be all, sir?' she asked primly.

He nodded and she went out, careful to close the door quietly behind her. His first weekend had come to an end. Thank goodness nothing had gone wrong. She only hoped she would be able to say the same when next Monday dawned.

She was eating her own egg when she heard the car

47

revving up in the garage. Within a few moments all was quiet and she went back into the breakfast-room. There was no need for her to have come in here again—she would leave the tray for the maid to clear—but curiosity had made her do so and she looked at the napkin folded on the table, the knife set on the plate and the silver lid replaced on the marmalade jar. Mr. Allen did not only require tidiness in others, he was equally tidy himself. 'A paragon of virtue,' she muttered, and walked out.

On Tuesday morning she checked with his secretary to confirm the names of the weekend guests. As well as the Godericks, there were a Mr. and Mrs. Frankenheim from Texas and a Lady Wittle who would be acting as hostess.

Anthea was startled by the curiosity this raised in her, and a quick glance through the guest book showed that Lady Wittle was an even more frequent visitor here than the Godericks. Again she was annoyed for not having spoken to Mrs. Goodbody about this guest book. Still, having assumed Mr. Allen to be a crotchety old man, it would not have entered her mind to find out whether he had any romantic interest in his life, nor to care even if he had. Not that she was interested now, she told herself. Her curiosity only stemmed from curiosity. The thought made her grin.

'You're a nosey parker, Anthea my girl,' she said aloud, and deliberately put all thoughts of her employer and his friends out of her mind.

On Thursday Monsieur Marcel, the French chef, arrived from London. He was a nattily dressed little man and drove a Renault shooting brake from which he unloaded basket after basket of provisions.

Within an hour he had taken control of the kitchen and Anthea, apprehensive as to how Mrs. Leggat would react, heaved a sigh of relief when the woman discarded her apron and retired to spend the weekend at her sister's cottage, leaving her husband—who was the butler—to perform his usual duties.

Surprisingly, Monsieur Marcel was not a temperamental chef—apart from the idiosyncrasy of bringing with him all his own knives—but glimpsing him at work as he cut and chopped and peeled, Anthea appreciated why he did so.

'Mr. Allen has given me a list of the wines he wants,' the Frenchman said, handing her a typewritten sheet of paper. 'But he's leaving the choice of soft drinks to you.'

'I'll pick vintage orange 1960!' she grinned, and handed the list to Leggat. 'Shall we go to the wine cellar now?'

The butler nodded, and feeling like a true châtelaine, Anthea went down to the basement—as clean here as the rest of the house—and unlocked a heavy oak door. Here were row after row of wines; all in racks, all stored at the correct temperature: not too warm to spoil the white and not too cold to spoil the reds.

Gently she and Leggat carried the necessary bottles up to the butler's pantry, where they would be decanted in good time and poured into beautiful crystal glass decanters.

'What about the soft drinks?' she enquired.

The butler smiled. 'That was Mr. Allen's little joke. Probably his way of telling you not to worry about anything.'

Doubtful that this was the reason—she saw her employer's remark more as sarcasm than reassurance—Anthea diplomatically held her tongue. It would not do to disclose her feelings about Mr. Allen to anyone else, particularly members of the staff.

On Friday afternoon she arranged all the flowers. It was luxurious to be able to go to the huge greenhouses and choose from a magnificent assortment of blooms, and she spent a long time there before coming away with several laden baskets. Mr. Allen preferred plants to cut flowers in the hall and library—again she gave thanks to the notes she

49

had made during her first week here with Mrs. Good-body—and she ordered the gardener to bring in pots of hydrangeas, bright green bamboo and darker leaved palms.

At five-thirty she had arranged both flowers and plants to her satisfaction, and went to her room to change into her party black. It was still two sizes too large and had a bunchy skirt and white collar and cuffs. Sturdy black shoes and thick stockings successfully spoiled her long and lovely legs, and beige powder and mauve lipstick immediately aged her ten years, making her look so plain that she burst out laughing.

She was hovering in the hall when the first guests arrived. They were Mr. and Mrs. Frankenheim, she with silver blue hair and silver mink coat, he wreathed in cigar smoke and aggressively new tweeds.

Hardly had she shown them to their room when Lady Wittle arrived, driving herself in a small and ancient car. She was not a day younger than seventy, and like Anthea made no concession to fashion, though her suit and brogues were obviously part of her character and not a disguise. She was tall and thin, with a strong face and a full lower lip similar to Mark Allen's, who Anthea learned with swiftly concealed astonishment was Lady Wittle's nephew.

'Either that young man gets married soon and has a wife to act as his hostess, or he'll have to find someone in place of *me*,' she said cheerfully as she gave Anthea a hearty handshake and stomped up the stairs to the room she knew was always hers. 'Who's here this weekend?'

Anthea told her and Lady Wittle grunted. 'Do the Frankenheims look as if they play bridge?'

'I can't tell,' Anthea replied, 'but Mr. and Mrs. Goderick do.'

'Claudine never plays cards when she's here. She's always too busy with my nephew. Is there anyone else coming?'

50

'Those are the only guests.'

'Well, I've brought a good book with me, so I can always read.'

'I'm sure you'll find Mrs. Frankenheim amusing and friendly.'

'How old is she?'

'About sixty.'

'That should put Claudine in a good mood. She can be a real bitch if she thinks she has any competition!'

Anthea moved to the door and Lady Wittle chuckled. 'I see you don't like gossiping, Miss Wilmot. You don't only look the perfect housekeeper, you act it!'

Anthea flushed and turned to regard the older woman, surprising a look of amusement on the lined face.

'How do you like working here?' Lady Wittle continued.

'I'm only here until Miss Evans is well enough to take up the position.'

'So my nephew told me.'

Anthea was surprised that Mr. Allen had bothered to talk to his aunt about his housekeeper, though the surprise was less pleasurable as the woman continued.

'He is rather doubtful about your being able to manage. Acts younger than the experience she says she has but looks older than her years, was the way he put it!'

Anthea fled before Lady Wittle came out with any more indiscretions, though the chuckle as she closed the door told her that the woman had enjoyed teasing her. If Lady Wittle behaved this way to everyone, the weekend might be more interesting than she had expected. Yet somehow she could not believe Mark Allen would have an indiscreet woman to act as his hostess, and a little later, as she saw her deep in conversation with the American couple, she knew she was right.

The Godericks had not yet arrived and it was Leggat who told her they usually drove down with Mr. Allen in his Rolls.

'There's talk of Mr. Goderick merging his business with Mr. Allen,' he added, 'and they've certainly been spending a lot of time together in the last few months.'

There were many questions Anthea would have liked to ask, but she had made a vow not to show any curiosity over her employer's behaviour, and she quickly changed the subject. However, it didn't stop her from remaining within earshot as his car glided to a stop in the drive at six-thirty that evening.

The other guests were in the drawing-room and she stood in the well of the stairs, ready to assign the Godericks to their respective suite.

Jasper Goderick came in first, a wizened man of indeterminate age with a wrinkled brown face and sparse hair. He had bright brown eyes that darted curiously around like a bird's, and a birdlike way of walking: quick jerky steps. But his voice was deep and booming, as if he had a built-in microphone in his throat.

Expecting his wife to be his contemporary, her appearance was a shock, for she was considerably younger and extremely beautiful: so beautiful that she took Anthea's breath away. Short black hair—as black as Mark Allen's own—curled riotously around her head, wisping on her forehead and over her shell-like ears. She had a small, full mouth, a delicate, straight nose and huge blue eyes. She looked as French as her christian name implied, though she was much taller than Frenchwomen normally were, and walked with an easy loping grace which wasn't French at all. A sensuously beautiful woman who also looked as though she enjoyed the outdoor life, Anthea thought with an inward frown. It seemed as if Claudine Goderick had everything. Not quite everything, Anthea amended as she saw the look that flashed on the girl's face as her husband's hand clutched possessively at her arm.

'Would you like to go upstairs?' Mark Allen was asking

his guests. 'Or do you want to come in and meet the Frankenheims first? My aunt you already know.'

'I'd like to meet the Frankenheims.' Jasper spoke before his wife could do so. 'That's the whole purpose of the weekend, isn't it?'

'You know it is,' Claudine said, only just managing to rob her words of sarcasm.

Her husband tilted his head and looked at her. She was several inches taller than he was but made no concession to this, for her heels were as high as fashion allowed. Lovely legs too, Anthea noted, and wished she could find something about Claudine that wasn't eye-catching.

'I think *I*'ll go to my room anyway,' Claudine said, and glanced at the black-clad figure standing by the stairs.

'My new housekeeper,' Mark Allen said, intercepting her glance and moving over with Claudine as she approached Anthea. 'Good evening, Miss Wilmot. Is everything all right?'

'Yes, thank you, Mr. Allen.'

Holding herself stiffly, Anthea led the way up the stairs. Mrs. Goderick obviously knew which room she had, for she walked directly to it as they reached the corridor.

'So Mrs. Goodbody has finally left?' she remarked.

'Only because her daughter needed her.'

'How boring to be a housekeeper all your life.' Blue eyes glanced curiously at Anthea. 'Are you Austrian, Miss Wilmot?'

'No,' Anthea said in surprise. 'Why do you ask?'

'You look it. I suppose it's because of your plaits and dirndl dress.'

Anthea tugged at her bunchy skirt and hid a smile. 'I wear what's practical, Mrs. Goderick. I have no time for fashion.'

'How wise of you. Life is so much easier if you don't.' She glanced at two large pigskin cases which Elsie, the

53

maid, was at that moment unpacking. 'What has Mr. Allen arranged for the weekend?' she asked casually.

'I don't know,' said Anthea, and remembered just in time to add the word "Madam". 'I believe Mr. Frankenheim will be going riding tomorrow, but——'

'Oh, I always do that when I'm here,' Claudine interrupted. 'I just wondered if anything else had been laid on—apart from Lady Wittle trying to inveigle me into one of her endless bridge games.'

Anthea chuckled, but as she saw the blue eyes widen, she set her lips together and put a forbidding frown on her face.

'Lady Wittle did mention something about bridge,' she said lugubriously, and went to the door. 'If there's anything else you require, Mrs. Goderick, please ask Elsie.'

A casual wave of the hand was her only reply, for the girl was busy examining her face in the dressing-table mirror. 'Run my bath,' she ordered Elsie, 'and then get out my black chiffon.'

Feeling like one of the Ugly Sisters, Anthea went down to the kitchen. It was amusing to play the part of a frump in front of an unsuspecting man but not quite so amusing to maintain the disguise when faced with a beautiful woman of her own age. But age was the only thing she and Claudine Goderick had in common. In every other respect they were worlds apart.

CHAPTER FIVE

Anxious for nothing to spoil the weekend, Anthea personally supervised everything. She knew she was being unnecessarily fussy but was determined not to give her employer any cause to complain about the way she carried out her duties. It was not so much because she wanted to keep the job for Betsy as a determination not to give him the satisfaction of being able to tell her she was no good, which she suspected he would dearly like to do.

Her disguise might have added ten years to her age, but in his eyes she was still too inexperienced for this job, and occasionally during the weekend she saw him watching her, a curious expression in his eyes as though he found her puzzling but did not know why.

She gave him full marks for perspicacity, realising somewhat wryly that his business success was based on his judgment. It was a good thing he only stayed at Bartham Manor for the weekends. If he were here the whole time she had a nervous suspicion he would quickly see through her.

On Sunday afternoon Mr. and Mrs. Frankenheim left, soon followed by Lady Wittle, who brusquely announced that her nephew did not need her to act as hostess for such good friends as the Godericks.

'It's unnecessary for Mark to bother you at all,' Anthea, who was hovering in the hall, heard Claudine say. 'He knows very well I'd be delighted to act as his hostess.'

'Mark doesn't feel it would be right to impose on another man's wife.'

'He's too old-fashioned,' Claudine retorted.

'You'd do well to remember that, my dear.' There was a glint in Lady Wittle's eye; a glint that was still there as she sought Anthea out in the housekeeper's sitting-room before she finally left.

'You did very well, Miss Wilmot. I thought you'd like to know that my nephew is delighted.'

'It's Monsieur Marcel and Leggat who deserve the credit,' Anthea replied.

'Don't be so modest! You arranged the flowers beautifully, and Mark said it was particularly clever of you to have changed Saturday's menu.'

'I was a bit worried about that,' Anthea admitted. 'But the head gardener's brother came down from Scotland with a fresh salmon and it seemed a shame to put it in the deep freeze. So we put the fillet steaks in there instead!'

'The salmon was superb,' Lady Wittle enthused, 'and the sauce was out of this world.'

'So it should have been. It was made with champagne.'

'Don't tell me Marcel is giving you his secrets?'

'It's *my* secret, actually,' Anthea grinned. 'I gave *him* the recipe!'

Lady Wittle registered astonishment. 'Don't tell me cooking is yet another of your virtues?'

'Another?' Anthea smiled.

'I'm sure you have many!' The woman held out her hand. 'Goodbye, Miss Wilmot. I know we'll be meeting again.'

No sooner had she gone when Leggat came in to say the Godericks had also decided to leave.

'Mr. Goderick is another one for early morning meetings,' the butler explained, 'and as his wife doesn't like getting up at the crack of dawn, they're going tonight. Quite put out she was at having to go.'

'Won't they be staying for dinner, then?' Anthea asked, cutting short the gossip, and as Leggat shook his head, she added: 'In that case you can put back the bottles of claret.'

'I've already decanted one.'

'What a waste!'

'Mr. Allen will kill the best part of it,' the butler replied, 'and I'll see there's a glass left for you!'

'Don't corrupt me,' Anthea smiled, and wondered whether Mrs. Goderick would come and say goodbye to her.

But she and her husband left without a word to the staff, though when Leggat came into the sitting-room again he was holding a ten-pound note.

'For all of us,' he said, waving it in the air. 'Mrs. Goodbody used to put all the tips in the cash box and divide it at the end of each month.'

'Then I'll do the same,' said Anthea, and locked it away. She had no intention of accepting anything for herself from Mr. Allen's guests, but would put the money aside for Betsy.

'Is Monsieur Marcel leaving for London tonight as well?' she asked.

Leggat nodded and grinned. 'He's packing his knives now! I thought of going into the village myself, once Mr. Allen has had supper.'

'You might as well go now,' said Anthea. 'You've been run off your feet the whole weekend.'

'This weekend is nothing compared with what it sometimes is. I think I'll stay and serve Mr. Allen first.'

'There's no need. It's all cold, so he'll probably help himself. Do go off for a few hours. If Mr. Allen requires anything, *I* can always see to it.'

Smiling his thanks, the butler went away, and Anthea wandered into the kitchen to say goodbye to the chef. In the short space of a couple of days she and the Frenchman had become firm friends, and she had enjoyed watching him work, learning more from his preparation of a couple of meals than she had learned from watching Chrissy for years.

'If you ever wish to train as a cook,' he said as he left, 'let me know and I will train you myself!'

'I may take you up on that one day,' she grinned, and thought it could well prove more rewarding than trying to teach history to uninterested youngsters.

By the time she returned to her sitting-room she was glad of a chance to sit down and relax. She would take the day off tomorrow and go and see her father. During the months of his illness they had grown very close and she still missed not seeing him every day. It was a closeness which might never be re-established and the knowledge depressed her. He had Maude for companionship now and did not need his daughter. Anthea sighed. Never in a million years would she have imagined her father falling in love with someone like Maude. Love must be blind, she decided, and suddenly saw an image of Claudine and Jasper Goderick. He certainly loved his beautiful wife; it was obvious from the way his eyes followed her everywhere she went; the way his hands reached out to touch her whenever she came near him. But the motive that had prompted Claudine to marry *him* had not stemmed from a similar emotion. Money seemed the obvious reason. Money to buy the expensive clothes that adorned her body and the magnificent jewellery that clasped her beautiful throat and arms. Yet Mr. Goderick, clever and astute though he was, still loved her.

The sharp buzz of a bell startled Anthea out of her reverie. It was the first time Mr. Allen had rung for her, and sticking a stray hairpin into her plaits she hurried to answer him.

He was in the small dining-room, looking at the laden table with acute dislike.

'The one thing Mrs. Goodbody forgot to tell you,' he said as she came in, 'is that I hate being fattened up like a calf for Christmas! For heaven's sake, have half that food taken away.'

Quickly Anthea went to do as he said and he gave an exclamation of annoyance.

'Not you, Miss Wilmot. It's Leggat's job. Anyway, why didn't *he* come when I rang?'

'He's off for the evening.'

'He has no business to go out while I'm still here. Damn it all, he does nothing all week when I'm in town!'

'It's my fault, sir,' Anthea said quickly. 'He didn't want to go, but I told him he could.'

58

'He should have known better than to listen to you. He's been with me long enough to know the service I expect.'

The comment was justified though the criticism was not, for Anthea felt she was solely to blame for the butler's absence. But when she tried to say so, Mark Allen cut her short.

'You've already made that point,' he said irritably, and watched as she started to remove some of the food.

'I suppose it will be thrown out,' he continued abruptly. 'I hate having food wasted.'

'It won't be wasted with all the staff we have,' she assured him, and went to the door with the tray. 'I'll come back for the rest in a moment, sir.'

'No, put it back!' As she stared at him he came over and took the tray from her. 'It's as heavy as lead,' he muttered, and banged it down on the table. 'You have no business lifting this.'

'I wanted to get it out of your way.'

'Are you as scared of me as you sound, Miss Wilmot?' His irritability had vanished and there was amusement in his soft voice.

'There's a difference between being scared of one's employer and wishing to please him,' she said coldly.

'Well, you will please me very much by sitting down and sharing my supper with me.'

Unsure that she had heard him correctly, she remained standing.

'Sit down,' he said testily. 'Or do you want me to hold the chair out for you?'

Scarlet-faced, she collapsed into a chair, and he immediately sat down opposite her.

'Help yourself to some meat, Miss Wilmot. I'm sure you don't need me to sell you the food? You probably prepared it yourself.'

'Monsieur Marcel did it.'

59

'Good for him,' came the sarcastic rejoinder. 'I was afraid you'd sent him off for a rest too. One day I anticipate coming down here to find everyone off on an extended holiday!'

'Leggat has only gone to the village to collect his wife,' she retorted. 'You make it sound as if he's gone on a world cruise!'

'I'm trying to make you realise that when I pay people to do a job, I expect them here to do it. I've never been accused of turning my servants into slaves—which your care for their wellbeing seems to indicate!'

'Oh no!' Anthea was horrified that her actions had been misjudged. 'It's just that it's such a waste of time for lots of people to hang around waiting on one man.' Colour swept into her face again. 'Oh dear,' she cried, 'now I really have put my foot in it.'

'Both of them,' he replied. 'You wouldn't be a communist, by any chance?'

'Certainly not! I just don't like to see people wasting their time.'

'My staff don't think they waste their time. They believe they have well paid jobs that aren't too difficult. If they didn't like it here, they wouldn't stay.' He helped himself to some cold meat and salad. 'Does your concern for my employees' waste of time extend to yourself?'

'No, sir. I have many things to keep me occupied.'

'Those ponderous volumes you consume by the dozen?'

'I enjoy reading. It stops me from being——' Her voice faltered, but he finished the sentence for her.

'It stops you from being bored to death?'

'I never said so.'

'Sometimes, Miss Wilmot, your expression speaks for you!' He set down his fork and looked at her. 'For such a self-controlled woman, you disclose a great deal about yourself without being aware of it.'

She wondered when he had had the chance to study her, and the question was answered as he continued: 'I've been watching you with my visitors and my aunt. You behaved differently with each one of them. Which reminds me— Claudine left this for you. She didn't want to give it to Leggat. She says it's for you personally.'

He took a five-pound note from his pocket and Anthea's face flamed.

'I'm not in the habit of accepting tips, Mr. Allen.'

'Staff do. It's one of the reasons they like their employers to give parties.'

The truth of his statement was undeniable and she knew she was foolish to feel resentful at Mrs. Goderick's gesture. She wished she could tell him her true background. After all, he knew she was only working here as a stand-in for Miss Evans and he must surely have wondered what she normally did with herself. But even as she opened her mouth to speak, she shut it again. The background of his housekeeper—especially a temporary one—was the last thing in the world he would be interested in knowing.

'Do you wish me to return the money to Mrs. Goderick?' he enquired, holding it up again.

'That would be rude,' Anthea said composedly, and taking the note from him, put it in her pocket.

'I'm glad to see you don't intend slipping it into your corselet.'

She looked at him, startled, then saw the gleam in his eyes—or was it the reflection of the light on his glasses? 'I don't wear one,' she said coolly. 'They went out with the dodo.'

'So has the get-up *you*'re wearing.'

She caught her breath. 'Mrs. Goodbody wore the same sort of dress.'

'Mrs. Goodbody had thirty years on you.'

A quick piece of mental arithmetic told Anthea he still

believed her to be in her middle thirties. It was a depressing thought, though a triumph to her disguise.

'I'll be quite happy to wear a different sort of uniform, sir.'

'I don't want you to wear a uniform at all! This isn't an institution, you know, it's my home!'

'I can wear another colour,' she said cautiously.

He shrugged, as though bored by the conversation, and picking up his fork resumed eating.

Manfully Anthea did the same. She usually had a hearty appetite, but tonight it seemed to have disappeared, no doubt due to the embarrassment she felt at sitting opposite this difficult man. Still, he was a mortal like herself. It was ridiculous to let his wealth and position turn her into a bundle of nerves.

Resolutely she helped herself to some more meat. It was certainly nicer to eat here than in the housekeeper's sitting-room. She still could not think of it as her own domain, though perhaps this was because she knew she was only here for a short time. How would it feel to have a permanent job like this one? It would give her sufficient free time to pursue any other subject in which she was interested. She could not see her father being pleased at the idea—he would consider it a waste of her academic talents—and her stepmother would be totally disapproving. She grinned at the thought of Maude.

'What's the joke?' her employer asked.

'I—er—something personal.'

'I'm glad to hear you have something personal to smile about. You seem so reserved, I was beginning to wonder if you had any personal thoughts whatever.'

'Do you always judge a book by its cover?'

'If it's a feminine book. Your fair sex are far more interested in cover than content!' He eyed her ugly black dress with disfavour. 'Not that you appear to be of similar mind.'

'I'll buy a more summery dress on my day off,' she said promptly. 'When you come down next weekend, you won't see me in black.'

'I may be going to Deauville with Mr. and Mrs. Goderick next weekend.'

'Isn't it rather dreary out of season?'

'It's even worse *in* season!' He helped himself to a liberal portion of trifle. 'Actually the season has already begun there. Mrs. Goderick wouldn't be going otherwise.'

'She loves showing off.' His glasses glinted and she added hastily: 'I mean, she's extremely beautiful, isn't she?'

'Extremely.'

His tone gave nothing away, and fearing she had said too much she lapsed into silence.

'My aunt liked you,' he said unexpectedly.

'I liked her,' Anthea said warmly, 'though she wasn't what I had expected.'

'What did you expect?'

'When I heard she was coming as your hostess, I thought she was ... I imagined she'd be....' Anthea drew a deep breath. 'I hadn't realised she was your aunt.'

'I would never allow a girl-friend to act as my hostess,' he said matter-of-factly. 'It might give her the wrong idea.'

'Wrong idea?'

'Marriage. That's one kind of partnership I'm not interested in.'

'Do you intend to remain a bachelor all your life?'

'Not all of it,' he said. 'I would like children. All this—' he waved his hand round the room—'would be pointless otherwise. But unfortunately one cannot have a family without the encumbrances that go with it.'

'And you regard a wife as an encumbrance?'

'I do.' His look was sardonic. 'There's no point in asking if you feel the same way about a husband. Most women see

63

marriage as the be-all and end-all of their existence.'

'For heaven's sake!' She caught herself up. 'I'm sorry, Mr. Allen. I shouldn't have said that.'

'Don't apologise, Miss Wilmot. You are dining at my table and there's no reason why you shouldn't talk to me on equal terms.'

'We can never be equal, Mr. Allen. Your whole way of living is alien to mine. You've devoted yourself to amassing money; you have no existence outside of that.'

'Would you find it more laudable if I spent my life in the hallowed precincts of Oxbridge and devoted myself to petty quarrels with fellow dons?'

Against her will Anthea burst out laughing—a warm sound that bubbled from her throat. He gave her a surprised glance, and as she became aware of it she sobered instantly and busied herself by picking up the plates and depositing them on the sideboard.

'Have you always been a housekeeper?' he asked slowly.

'I've always kept house,' she replied, keeping her back to him. 'My mother died when I was a child and I looked after my father.'

'What does he do?'

She pretended not to hear him. 'Would you like your coffee now, Mr. Allen, or later?'

'Now.' He watched in silence as she poured it out and brought him a cup. 'Join me,' he said laconically, and again she did as he bid.

He sat quietly sipping it, looking unexpectedly tired. After the busy week he had spent in London, it would have done him more good to have had a quiet weekend and not one devoted to business. She knew from what Leggat had told her that he had been closeted until the small hours with Mr. Goderick and Mr. Frankenheim. But she did not have the right to tell him he was overworking; nor did anyone else, for that matter, if what he had said earlier was true.

64

He was a loner who enjoyed living his life this way.

As though aware of her scrutiny he moved his head in her direction, and the heavy rims of his glasses gave him a forbidding air.

'How long is your friend likely to be ill, Miss Wilmot?'

'Betsy, you mean? I hope she'll be able to come here in a couple of months; perhaps a little earlier.'

'Do you have another job to go to?'

'Not until October,' she said quickly.

'Is it near here?'

'Not far away.'

'You seem to like this district.'

'I've lived in this area all my life.' She hesitated. 'Where were you born, Mr. Allen?'

'In this house.' He saw her amazement and grinned wickedly. 'Did you think mine was a rags to riches story? I'm sorry to disappoint you, Miss Wilmot, but my background is considered to be impeccable. Poor but impeccable.'

She glanced around her. 'Hardly poor, Mr. Allen.'

'The house was all we had. Two world wars killed off the senior males in the family and death duties crippled my father. When I was seven we sold up and moved to London.'

She was startled and unable to hide it. 'But how did you ... I mean, you. ...'

'I was able to retrieve the family fortunes,' he said blandly, 'and buy back the house when it came on the market again.'

'You're lucky it did. It's a lovely place. I can't imagine anyone wanting to sell it.'

He laughed again, and white teeth flashed in a tanned face, making him look Italian. 'When I bought out Hercules Holdings, this house was the home of its chairman!' He glanced around him. 'I keep meaning to change the furnishings, but I haven't got round to it yet.'

'A wife would do it for you,' she said demurely.

'So would an interior decorator—and far less expensive in the long run!'

Anthea smiled. He had a dry sense of humour that appealed to her. 'What is your ambition now, Mr. Allen, or have you achieved everything you want?'

'Does one ever achieve everything one wants?'

She thought of her father, content with his books and his second marriage. 'I think so,' she murmured. 'Some people do.'

'I wish I was one of them. Unfortunately I'm the driver driven.'

'I don't follow that.'

He shrugged. 'I'm driven by restlessness and that forces me into activity which makes me force others into activity too.'

'Have you never been able to relax?'

'A long time ago I could.' He stood up and began to pace the room. 'Not any more, though. It's boredom, Miss Wilmot. I do it all because of boredom.'

'You mean poverty of inner resources, Mr. Allen.'

'You have a sharp turn of phrase, Miss Wilmot! It doesn't go with your hausfrau appearance.' His words reminded her of her position and she stood up.

'Would you care for another cup of coffee, sir?' And then as he shook his head: 'In that case, perhaps you'll excuse me?'

'Of course. It was remiss of me to keep you talking so late.'

She glanced at her wristwatch and saw it was nearly eleven. Time had flown without her noticing it.

'My secretary will let you know if I'll be here next weekend,' he said, and murmured goodnight before she reached the door.

66

As she went to her bedroom she tried not to be resentful of his casual dismissal; after all, she had been the one to suggest ending the evening; but she wished he had not accepted it with such alacrity. Seeing her reflection in her dressing-table mirror she giggled. No wonder he had not wanted to extend their conversation together. It was amazing he had wanted to begin it in the first place.

She took off her steel-rimmed spectacles, then took out her hairpins and shook her head. The chestnut brown plait fell past her shoulders and she undid it and started to brush it free. How much younger she looked with her hair a satin curtain round her face, and what a ridiculous contrast it was to this bunchy black dress. Tomorrow she would go into Reading and buy herself a less hideous one. Inexplicably she thought of Claudine Goderick's exquisite clothes and shook her head. Jasper was too high a price to pay for them. No amount of money could ever be compensation for spending one's life with a man one did not love. And if one did fall in love, then the money he had would be unimportant. What a pity that Mr. Allen was too cynical to believe a woman could think that way.

CHAPTER SIX

As he had half indicated, Mark Allen went to Deauville the following weekend, a fact reported in the gossip columns of the tabloid which Mrs. Leggat avidly read each morning. Surprisingly there was also a picture of him taken with Claudine Goderick, the caption beneath it implying that the couple were going away together for the weekend. In the fuller blurb written below, however, Jasper Goderick was stated to be in the party, and described as a wiry Australian.

'He doesn't have an Australian accent,' Mrs. Leggat muttered, and her husband nodded sagely.

'Because he's lived here the best part of his life. Here and in Canada. That's where he met his wife.'

'Let's hope she remains *his* wife,' Mrs. Leggat frowned at the photograph of Claudine. 'I wouldn't fancy having her as mistress here.'

Anthea's ears pricked, but she forcibly reminded herself of her determination not to gossip. Happily her conscience was appeased and her curiosity satisfied as Leggat himself continued the conversation.

'If Mr. Allen has managed to avoid matrimony so far, he won't succumb to Mrs. Goderick.'

'His other women friends haven't been like *her*,' Mrs. Leggat snorted. 'She's a very determined woman.'

'So is her husband. He watches her like a hawk.'

'I'm not surprised. Any man who marries someone young enough to be his daughter is asking for trouble!'

'They've been happily married for eight years,' the butler protested. 'I heard Mr. Goderick say so at dinner the other night.'

'It won't last another eight,' Mrs. Leggat prophesied. 'Not now she's met Mr. Allen.'

Anthea rustled the notebook in her hand. She had come in to make a list of the provisions that needed to be re-ordered and felt it would be better to put an end to his conversation. Taking the hint, Mrs. Leggat went into the larder, and for the next hour the two of them concentrated on the stock cupboard.

Later that day, as Anthea drove to her father's house—odd that she did not think of it as her own home any more—she wondered how accurate Mrs. Leggat's gossip was about Mr. Allen and the lovely Claudine.

It did not require great acumen to know that the girl did not love her husband. It was apparent in the cool way she

68

spoke to him and the derisive looks she gave him when he was not looking in her direction, and which had been one of the first things Anthea had noticed. Yet she did not have much sympathy for Jasper Goderick either. He was too wily a bird not to know the character of the girl he had married nor her reasons for marrying him. Money! Anthea thought scornfully. It made women want men and men want the world. But what an empty world it often turned out to be for them. Mark Allen had said so himself. He had all the money he was ever likely to need, yet he was bored. What greater indictment could there be against the ambitious striving for wealth and business success?

Thoughts of her employer turned her to thoughts of the promise she had made him to wear something more cheerful, and that afternoon she went to a store and searched along the racks. There were plenty of pretty dresses, but regretfully she passed them by, and emerged from the shop with a hideous floral print that she could not wait to wear. What would he say when he saw her in it? A smile tugged at the corners of her mouth and she was so deep in thought that she bumped into a man coming out of a newsagent's.

'Anthea!' he exclaimed. 'I've been trying to contact you for a fortnight. Where on earth have you been?'

It was Roger Pemberton, a young sociologist at the University whom she had met through her father. For more than a year he had pursued her, blindly ignoring her repeated warnings that she did not love him.

'Your stepmother told me you were working for Mark Allen,' he said, falling into step beside her. 'Does that mean you aren't coming back to get your degree?'

'Of course not. I've only taken the job for a few months.'

'Tell me about it over coffee,' he said, and propelled her into a nearby café.

Sitting opposite him at a window table, Anthea gave him a guarded reason for leaving home, stressing her desire to be independent as well as to give her father and his bride a chance of being alone.

'Don't tell me sixty-year-olds need to be left on their own?' Roger expostulated.

'Wait till you're sixty,' she teased.

'If I go on chasing you, it looks as if I might have to!'

'That's why I keep telling you to find someone else.'

'I don't want anyone else.' He was suddenly serious. 'What's wrong with me, Anthea? All the other girls I know seem to like me.'

'I like you too. But I don't love you.'

'Are you in love with anyone else?'

'No.'

'Then I won't stop trying. How about coming to the cinema with me tonight? There's a Truffaut film showing.'

She accepted the invitation. She had not had more than a couple of afternoons off since she had started work, and with Mr. Allen in Deauville it seemed pointless to remain tied to the house.

'I'll be staying at home for a few days,' she told him. 'It seems ages since I've seen any of my friends.'

'It is ages,' he said plaintively. 'You must tell me when you're free and I'll drive over to see you.'

'You mustn't do that.' She was aghast at what he would make of her braided hair and outlandish clothes. 'Mr. Allen loathes visitors.'

'Really? I heard he was rather sociable. Some of his parties have——'

'They were for *his* friends,' she interrupted. 'He wouldn't feel the same having *my* friends calling round.'

'I'm sure you're exaggerating. If you live there, he can't expect you to be a recluse.'

'That was the understanding on which I went to work for him. That no one came to see me.'

'Then the quicker October comes, the better,' Roger said

grimly.

Maude Wilmot made a similar comment the following day when Anthea refused her offer to drive her back to Bartham Manor.

'Living alone on that estate is making you morbid,' she grumbled.

'I'm not alone,' Anthea said hastily. 'The place is teeming with servants.'

'That's hardly the same as having your friends and family around. Your father and I will come over to see you next week. I understand the gardens at the Manor are beautiful. Professor Jenkins's wife was telling me about it. She's a keen horticulturist and Mr. Allen's gardener occasionally takes her through the greenhouses.'

'I can easily fix that for you,' Anthea promised. 'I'll phone and tell you when to come.'

'We'll pop over one afternoon when the weather is good. It's only a short run by car.'

'Make it during the week,' Anthea said instantly. 'I'm generally busy on Saturday and Sunday.'

'That's the time most secretaries are free.'

'Weekends are the only time Mr. Allen can work with me.'

'Why doesn't he take you to London with him?'

'He's too busy to write there.' Anthea marvelled at her ability to lie. 'Don't forget this book is just a hobby for him. He doesn't want it to interfere with his other work.'

'You would have thought that someone in his position would take time off—if he's really serious about the book, of course.'

'He's extremely serious about it,' Anthea said, 'but when you run a financial empire you can't take time off whenever you like.'

Adjuring her stepmother once again not to come over and see her during a weekend, Anthea returned to the Manor.

As always her senses were stirred by the sight of its graceful lines and the beauty of its surroundings. What a pity that its interior was not equally lovely. It was ridiculous that Mark Allen did not find the time to furnish it the way it deserved. It was not even a question of time, she admitted, for as he himself had said, there was no shortage of interior decorators willing to do the work. If only she herself could be given the chance of doing it. Pushing the thought aside, she rearranged her packages more comfortably in her arms and walked round to the back of the house.

She stopped in surprise as she saw the garage doors open and the gleaming Rolls inside. She took a step towards it and then drew back with a gasp. Her hair was loose around her face and she was wearing her own clothes. If anyone saw her like this, the game would be up. Head bent low, she raced the rest of the way to the back door, and only when she reached the safety of her bedroom did she breathe a sigh of relief.

Her stepmother had been at home when she had left the house and because of this she had been forced to depart wearing one of her own jaunty outfits. She had planned to stop off at the local railway station and change into her disguise. But the fact that her employer had so far never returned to the Manor during the week had lulled her into security, and she had considered that the risk of being seen by anyone was so small that it did not justify the bother of changing until she reached the Manor.

With trembling hands she set down her parcels and unbuttoned her jacket. From now on this was a risk she dared not take. She would have to depart and arrive as the dowdy Miss Wilmot.

Quickly she plaited her hair and pinned it round her head, then scrubbed her face clean of make-up. Without mascara and darkened eyebrows she felt almost naked, while her lips were so pale that she bit them to give them more colour.

Unwrapping the parcel, she took out her new dress and hastily put it on. What a monster it was! Pink and yellow daisies fought madly with each other on a mud-brown background, the colour of which gave her skin a sallow tinge. As she had promised Mr. Allen, it did not have long sleeves but full puffed ones that reached just below her elbow—the most unflattering length she could find. The skirt was box-pleated and too large, and she was obliged to fold it double at the waist. This made it fall lumpily over her hips and added inches to them. But the bodice was the real *pièce de résistance*: pin-tucked and high-necked, with a Peter Pan collar embroidered with yellow and pink flowers, and large pink buttons shaped like daisies.

Pursing her mouth into a prim bow, she went down to the kitchen, managing with some effort to maintain her composure in the face of Mrs. Leggat's look of astonishment.

'All dressed up in your summer things, Miss Wilmot?' the woman said, hurriedly averting her face.

'I bought it yesterday,' Anthea answered brightly. 'It's very pretty, isn't it?'

'Yes, dear.' Mrs. Leggat was in control of her expression again and gave Anthea an appraising look.

Anthea stood her ground and stared back. It might not be difficult to fool Mark Allen, but it was not so easy to fool people whom she saw every day, particularly this woman, who had a sufficiently keen eye to see beyond the screwed-back hair and limp clothes. It would take more than a disguise to make the staff put her in the same class and age group as Mrs. Goodbody, and it said much for their kindliness that none of them had asked her what game she was playing or why she had accepted a job for which she had no training beyond a quick mind and the ability to learn fast.

'I'm surprised Mr. Allen didn't let us know he was

73

coming down,' she commented. 'I would have come back last night if I'd known.'

'There'd have been no need for you to do that,' Mrs. Leggat responded cheerfully. 'Besides, he only arrived this morning.'

'How long will he be staying?'

'Just tonight, I think.'

'I'd better go and see if he requires anything,' Anthea said, and went in search of him.

The dusk of early April had settled on the house, and wall sconces were already lit, softening the heavy furniture and sombre wallpaper. There was no sign of her employer, though she saw Leggat setting the table in the breakfast-room, and seeing her hovering in the hall, he pointed to the library.

She knocked on the door and, at Mark Allen's command, went in. He was standing by the window, looking out at the garden.

'Don't bother drawing the curtains yet, Leggat,' he said without turning round. 'I'll do it myself later. I always like this hour of the day.'

'It isn't Leggat, Mr. Allen, it's me, Miss Wilmot.'

At this he turned. With the window behind him his face was in darkness, but though she could not see his expression, there was no mistaking the convulsive movement of his shoulders as he took in her appearance. But when he spoke his voice was as mild as always, and again she was aware how different it was from his dynamic manner and appearance. Had he deliberately cultivated this quiet voice, or was it his aura which was the false part of him? Yet why should she suppose any part of him to be false? He had no need to pretend. He was rich enough to do as he wanted, when he wanted, regardless of what anyone else thought.

'I came in to see if you require anything, sir,' she said. 'We weren't expecting you until the weekend.'

'It was such a lovely day that I got fed up staying in town. If the weather holds, I'll be down tomorrow too.'

'Isn't it a long drive to do each day, sir?' she said, uncomfortably aware that his eyes had moved from the bodice to the hem of her dress and then back again.

'It's pretty quick on the motorway,' he replied. 'And with a tape and telephone in my car, my time isn't wasted.'

'It's a pity you haven't got a telex too.'

'That's a good idea. I hadn't thought of it.' His glasses glinted and she backed to the door.

With his eyes covered by his lenses he had an unfair advantage over her, and she wished her own steel-rimmed spectacles had thicker glass.

'I'm glad to see you've taken my advice,' he said suddenly.

She was so preoccupied with her own thoughts that she was caught out, 'Advice about what?'

'Buying yourself a prettier dress.'

Knowing he was lying in his back teeth, she determined to take his words at face value. 'It is pretty, isn't it?' She put a deep note of pleasure into her voice. 'I'm so glad you like it, sir.'

'I do indeed, Miss Wilmot. The daisies suit your personality.'

Wondering what a daisy personality was, Anthea slipped from the room, and was halfway across the hall when she remembered she had not found out if he wanted anything special to eat. But nothing would induce her to go back to the library, and she returned to her sitting-room. If he wanted anything he would demand it: of that she could be certain.

During the week, when the house was unoccupied except for the staff, Anthea had made it her duty to go through the main rooms herself each night to check that the windows were securely locked. This was part of Leggat's job, but she none the less double-checked, loath to have anything happen during her stay here.

That evening she automatically did the same, and was coming out of the drawing-room when her employer emerged from the library. He was wearing a silk dressing gown of an unusual Chinese design, and the rich red satin gave a pink tinge to his skin that made him look less forbidding.

'What are you doing here, Miss Wilmot?'

'Checking that the windows are locked.'

'When the burglar alarm is on, it's better to leave them unlocked.'

'Isn't that encouraging someone to come in?'

'They'll set up a hell of a racket if they do! Ever heard those alarms go off?'

'No,' she said quickly, 'and I hope I don't. I've a thing about burglars. Someone broke into our house one night when we were out and ransacked the place.' She shivered at the memory. 'Every cupboard and drawer had been tipped on the floor. They'd even gone through all my clothes.'

'That must have given them a thrill!'

She gave him a startled look and saw the colour come warmly into his face.

'Forgive me, Miss Wilmot, that was extremely uncalled-for on my part.'

'It certainly was,' she retorted primly. 'I'm sorry if my taste in clothes doesn't meet with your approval. But I never knew it was a prerequisite of my job.'

'Oh, come now,' he expostulated, 'I thought a woman is always flattered when a man takes an interest in her appearance.'

'I wear what I can afford,' she said aloofly, and with a toss of her head went down the hall and into the servants' quarters.

Mark Allen left before seven next morning, but this time Leggat was up to serve his breakfast and Anthea had just put in an appearance in the sitting-room when she heard the Rolls purr away.

It promised to be a lovely spring day, and after she had made her usual inspection of the house and spent an hour in the linen room with the seamstress who came once a month to do any necessary repairs, she changed into a sundress, took an armful of books and went to sit in the rose garden.

It was too early for flowers, but it was more secluded here than anywhere else, and she settled herself beneath an arbour and was soon absorbed in her reading.

She only returned to the house as the slanting rays of the sun cooled, and she was still in her bedroom when she heard a car coming along the drive. Her room was on the top floor, facing the front, unlike those of the other staff who occupied the west wing. But a housekeeper, she supposed, held a more privileged position, and she was glad of it, for it meant that from her windows she had a view of the distant river where an occasional boat could be seen breaking the glassy surface of the water.

She went to the window and peered down. Yes, it was the Rolls. Mr. Allen was back earlier than she had expected. Quickly she slipped off her sun-dress and reached for the floral one; shuddering as she saw the daisy-shaped buttons. Her hand was on the bodice when there was a knock at the door.

'Who is it?' she called.

'It's Elsie,' the Danish maid replied, and came in carrying a box. 'This is for you, Miss Wilmot. From the master.'

'For me?' Anthea took the box. It had a Fortnum & Mason label and, though large, was light in weight. 'You may go, Elsie,' she said, and waited till the door had closed before she undid the string.

Carefully she pulled aside the layers of tissue paper and shook out a silver-grey dress in heavy French

77

crêpe. Astounded, she stared at it, her thoughts so chaotic that they made no sense. But after a moment she started to smile and was still smiling as she put it on and regarded her reflection in the mirror. The dress was several sizes too large for her—as she had expected—for in trying to assess her size, Mark Allen had been fooled by the voluminous wrap-round folds of her own dresses. And thank goodness he *had* been fooled! If this new dress had actually fitted her, it would have put an end to her pretence. It was beautifully cut and styled, with a softly fitted collar, simple bodice, plain long sleeves and graceful gathered skirt. But because it was large and too long, it looked frumpish, and she deliberately increased this by making the belt at the waist even looser.

Chuckling audibly, she put on her usual thick black stockings, heavy lace-up shoes and old-fashioned spectacles, then clumped purposefully downstairs to thank him for his gift. Her hand clutched at the banisters. She sincerely hoped it was a gift. If he expected her to pay for it, she would be broke for a month.

'Of course it's a gift,' he said tersely when she searched him out and found him in the library. 'I thought you'd realise that without having to ask?'

'I'm not used to receiving things from my employers. It's most kind of you, sir.'

'I did it to please me, not you,' he said, and scowled at her.

'What's wrong?' she asked. 'Don't you like it?'

'Not as much as I thought I would,' he said candidly. 'There's something wrong with it.'

He was looking at the dress so intently that she knew it would not take him long to guess it was too big for her. Hurriedly she went to the door.

'Now where are you off to?' he called.

'The kitchen.'

78

'Don't go yet.' Restlessly he moved from his desk. 'What sort of a day has it been here?'

'Beautiful. I was working in the garden all the afternoon.'

'Don't tell me you're a gardener too?'

'Not that sort of work,' she smiled. 'I meant I was reading.'

'One of those weird books of yours?'

'A history book,' she corrected coldly.

'Can't you find anything more rewarding than the Life of Ethelred the Unready?'

'I enjoy history, sir. You obviously don't.'

'I'm more interested in the future than the past.'

'Knowing the past can frequently help one to assess what the future will hold.'

'Meaning that life is a circle and the same things recur?' He shook his head. 'I'm afraid I don't support that view, Miss Wilmot. Nothing remains the same; everything changes.'

'People don't. They go on making the same mistakes.'

His dark brows met in a frown and his glasses slipped down. He pushed them back. 'You're right in that respect, Miss Wilmot. Leopards don't change their spots either!'

'I wouldn't liken people to animals, sir.'

'Wouldn't you?' He frowned again. 'No, I wouldn't either. Animals are nicer!'

'Then you've been unlucky in your choice of friends,' she said before she could stop herself.

'I take it you don't like mine?'

'I haven't given them any thought,' she said untruthfully, and walked out with such a determined step that she knew he would think twice before calling her back.

After she had supper—taking it with Mrs. Leggat in her sitting-room—she was too restless to remain indoors, and slipping on a coat, went out for a walk.

It was cooler at this hour of the evening, and the air was damp from the river. Sinking her chin lower into her collar, she quickened her steps. Her employer's presence in the house had made her unaccountably edgy, and though she knew it was easy to avoid him, she could not as easily keep him from intruding into her thoughts.

Leaving the drive, she strode across the lawns until she reached the belt of trees that lay some quarter of a mile from the house. The young moon was riding high and everything was sharply etched in black and silver. It made the scene darker and somehow menacing, turning the tree-trunks to skeletons and the branches to writhing arms.

She took a step back and headed for the river. Behind her came the snap of a twig and she stopped, wondering if she had disturbed an animal. The sound came again. It was too heavy to come from scampering paws and she knew it was a person. She glanced over her shoulder. The house was out of sight and there was no place for her to hide between here and the main gate some hundred yards away. Smartly she started to walk in its direction, but the steps behind her came more quickly too and she began to run. So did her unknown pursuer. But he was running faster than she was, and the sound of his feet came closer and closer until he was directly behind her.

A hand came on her shoulder and she gave a scream and whirled round, the sound dying as she saw thick black hair and a tight set mouth.

'Why on earth were you running away from me?' Mark Allen demanded.

'I didn't know it was you.' She was gasping for breath and tried to gulp in more air.

He caught her by the elbow and pulled her along to a wooden bench, half hidden behind a clump of massive rhododendrons.

'If you'd had the sense to turn round,' he said, too angry

to be polite, 'you wouldn't have practically given yourself a heart attack!'

'I was afraid to turn in case it slowed me down. It never entered my head it was you.'

'I wasn't sure it was you, either,' he said, and she was suddenly conscious that she was wearing a good tweed coat, tightly belted to show her waist. But the hem of her dress was sticking out three inches below it, and this managed to minimise the smart line.

'I don't think it's wise for you to go out walking alone at night,' he went on. 'If you want some exercise, take one of the dogs with you.'

'That's a good idea. I'll take Judy.'

'She might not be amenable. She's the most difficult of the bunch.'

'We're friends,' Anthea explained. 'She regards me as her ballboy!'

He laughed. 'I'm glad you like Alsatians. Lots of people are afraid of them.'

'I used to have one,' she admitted. 'It died when I was fourteen.'

'They need a lot of exercise. It isn't fair to keep them in a small house.'

'We have a large garden.' She stopped abruptly. 'At least not large by your standards.'

'Are your parents still alive?'

'You've asked me that before. My mother is dead and my father remarried again at Christmas.'

'What does your father do?'

'You asked me that before, too.'

'You didn't answer me, if I remember rightly.' There was no masking the irony in his voice, and she knew she could not hedge this time.

'He teaches history.' It was the truth, though phrased in such a way as to give the wrong impression.

81

'So that's why you're so keen on the subject,' he said. 'You should have tried for university, Miss Wilmot. I'm a great believer in education.'

'Even for women?'

'Even for women.' This time he was smiling openly. 'Do I strike you as so old-fashioned that I would deny the female sex an education?'.

'I get the impression you don't give much thought to the female sex—in general, that is.'

'That's true,' he admitted. 'Though from time to time I think about the female sex in particular!' He crossed his arms on his chest and leaned against the bench, although he did not sit down. 'I've been giving *you* quite a bit of thought as it so happens, Miss Wilmot. You intrigue me.'

She looked down at the ground, staring at it as if she had never seen ground before.

'Well?' he said. 'Aren't you at least going to ask me why? You really are the least curious of women.'

Still she did not look up, and he gave a mocking sigh. 'I can see I'll have to tell you. You intrigue me because I suspect a very bright mind behind that servile exterior.'

'I'm never servile, Mr. Allen.'

'Perhaps servile is the wrong word. Maybe I mean deliberately deprecating. The way you keep calling me "sir", as if you need to establish my superiority.'

'I didn't think I needed to do the obvious!'

He gave a soft laugh. 'There you are! You've done it again.'

'Done what?'

'Shown me the edge of your sharp tongue and your agile brain.'

'It's just an ordinary brain,' she protested. 'I can't help it if you're used to dumb women.'

'They're not all dumb,' he said gently. 'Claudine is very bright.'

'She's sophisticated.' Anthea stood up. 'That isn't the same.'

'Tell me the difference.' He fell in step beside her as she started to walk back to the house.

'I would rather not discuss your friends, sir.'

'Then let's discuss yours,' he said. 'How come you aren't married, Miss Wilmot?'

'I should have thought that was obvious, sir. Men like pretty women.'

'What's wrong with you?'

'I can hardly be called pretty.'

'That's true,' he agreed at once. 'You're far too intelligent for me to lie to you. But you have an intriguing personality.'

He stopped walking and she was forced to do the same, trying to look unconcerned as she felt his eyes on her. Though the moonlight blanched everything of colour, it also obliterated the unbecoming beige powder which she effected, and threw into relief the clear lines of her face and delicate bone structure. She saw an odd look cross his face, a quick frown to be replaced almost immediately by puzzlement.

'You look different ... younger.'

'Moonlight hides my lines, sir.'

'You don't have any.'

'I'm older than you think, Mr. Allen.'

'I'm not sure what I think.' He continued to stare at her. 'There's something else about you. I'm not sure what, but—Darn it, I do know! You aren't wearing your glasses!'

With a gasp she put her hand to her face. She had slipped her glasses into her pocket when she had left the house, and had never given them another thought. But as she went to put them on, he stopped her.

'Do you have to wear them, Miss Wilmot? They don't

83

look strong lenses to *me*.'

Afraid he might snatch them from her and discover they were plain glass, she buried them deep into her pocket again.

'Good,' he replied, seeing the gesture as her answer. 'Don't wear them any more. You look much nicer without them.'

Purposefully Anthea began walking again, faster this time, and he was forced to keep in step with her.

'I'll be down tomorrow night,' he said. 'I work better here.'

'You bring work with you?'

'You don't think I just sit in the library in the evening and do nothing?' he asked with some amusement.

'I thought you listened to music and relaxed.'

'I'm in the middle of working out a very big merger, Miss Wilmot.' He frowned. 'I don't know why I told you that.'

'Perhaps you felt like talking about it. Talking is relaxing too.'

'The solicitous attention of a docile woman?' His laugh was sudden. 'I prefer to relax on a settee!'

'It's less of a commitment,' she agreed. 'You can always get up and walk away!'

'I do that from women too!'

Knowing that he did was somehow painful, and she said nothing.

'I'm going to have the house redecorated,' he remarked.

The allusion did not escape her and she could not prevent a slight chuckle.

'What's funny about that, Miss Wilmot?'

'I get the feeling you'd like to redecorate me too.'

'I tried,' he said, eyeing the hem of her dress. 'But it wasn't as successful as I had hoped.'

'You can't make a silk purse out of a sow's ear, sir,' she

replied, lids lowered to hide the sparkle in her eyes.

'So it would appear. Let's hope I'm luckier with the house.'

'Who's going to do it?'

'Jackson Pollard. He has an excellent reputation. I'm leaving it all to him.'

'Is that wise? You might find yourself with a showplace instead of a home.'

'Claudine's going to keep an eye on it for me, and she has excellent taste.'

Anthea was pleased she had not been stupid enough to offer her own services. Besides, how astonished he would have been if she had done so. What did a dowdy-looking spinster know about colour integration and decor?

'I will leave you here, Miss Wilmot,' he said unexpectedly. 'I fancy walking a bit more.'

Anthea nodded silently, then murmured goodnight as he moved away.

CHAPTER SEVEN

MARK ALLEN returned to the Manor every night that week. Anthea managed to keep out of his way after their encounter on Tuesday evening, though his presence continued to make her strangely restless.

He had not been joking when he said he brought back work with him, for she knew from Leggat that he rarely left the library until one or two in the morning, and he was up and on his way back to London by seven-thirty.

On Thursday and Friday she was on tenterhooks to know if he would have any guests for the weekend, and was relieved when Friday morning came and went without any word from his secretary. This meant he would be coming down alone, and she hoped he would have the sense to relax. She glanced through the notes she had made about him during her apprenticeship with Mrs. Goodbody, and arranged with Mrs. Leggat to prepare the dishes he liked best. They were simple ones, she noted with surprise: roast chicken with tarragon, rib of beef with Yorkshire pudding and fried Dover sole. Nothing esoteric here!

At midday on Friday a blue Mercedes disgorged a silver-haired man and his equally silver-haired assistant. It was Jackson Pollard, and he gave Anthea a letter from Mr. Allen's secretary requesting her to show him over the house and to answer all questions relating to Mr. Allen's habits.

'It's so important for me to understand my client and know what he likes,' he drawled, waving a languid hand, though his eyes were far from languid as they darted round him, sizing up the potential. 'Mr. Allen has given me carte blanche, but it still has to be his home.'

'Is Mrs. Goderick meeting you here today?' Anthea asked.

'No, no. She wants to see what colour schemes I choose, but first I have to prepare them. And before that, I must get to know the house.'

He began a systematic appraisal of it. Beneath his feminine manner there lay a hard streak of realism and a Birmingham accent which came out in the flat vowels and occasional slurring of words. The misgivings Anthea had felt at the sight of him abated as the afternoon proceeded, and she answered all his questions as candidly as she could. No, she had no idea if Mr. Allen spent a great deal of time in the bathroom nor if he preferred a shower. Yes, he did like to have his meals in the breakfast-room when he was alone, and yes, he was very fond of formal dinners when he was entertaining.

'A long dining-table, then,' Jackson Pollard decided. 'I have exactly the one to suit him. Maple wood—absolutely

86

divine!'

It was six o'clock by the time he left, and hardly had the car rolled down the drive when the Rolls purred up it. Quickly Anthea retreated down the hall. It was childish of her to keep on avoiding her employer. She would eventually have to see him for one reason or another, and the longer she put it off the more embarrassed she would be when it happened, even though it was difficult to know why she should be embarrassed at all. It certainly had nothing to do with his behaviour and stemmed only from her own emotions. Being alone so much was making her fanciful. It was time she saw something of her friends.

On an impulse she went into her sitting-room and dialled Roger Pemberton's flat. The bell rang several times and she felt relieved at getting no answer. It was unfair to ring him just because she had a fit of the blues.

She was in the act of putting down the receiver when it was lifted at the other end and Roger's voice came on the line. Deciding fate had made him answer, she gave him a bright greeting and said she was free on Monday, if he still wanted to see her.

'You bet!' he exclaimed. 'I'm free in the afternoon as well. I'll come and pick you up.'

Unwilling for him to see her disguise, she said a hasty no, and gave the excuse that she wanted to go home for a few hours first.

'Call for me between seven and half past,' she suggested, 'and I'll introduce you to my stepmama.'

'As your fiancé, I hope?'

'Not a chance,' she laughed, and said goodbye before he could prolong the conversation.

Her chat with Roger, though short, had cheered her up, and for the rest of the evening she felt in a considerably better mood. She could even look at herself in the mirror without a shudder.

For the whole of Saturday Mark Allen remained in the library, his desk—so Leggat informed her—covered with a mass of documents. He had his lunch there as well, asking for sandwiches so that he could eat with the minimum of fuss.

In the evening he ordered sandwiches again, and Anthea, talking to Mrs. Leggat in the kitchen, was overcome by anger. How could he be content with makeshift meals when there was so much delicious food prepared and waiting in the refrigerator?

'Don't bother with sandwiches,' she said sharply. 'I'm going in to talk to him.'

'He'll bite your head off,' Leggat warned.

'I'll bite him back!' she snapped, and went out.

But the sight of him at his desk, his hair awry, the yellow of fatigue staining his skin, robbed her of temper and reminded her that as his employee she had no right to criticise or tell him what to do.

'Yes,' he said wearily. 'What do you want?'

'Merely to let you know that Mrs. Leggat has prepared your favourite dinner, sir. She'll be most upset if you don't have it.'

'Mrs. Leggat can go to Hades! I'm busy, Miss Wilmot.' He bent to his papers, but as if aware that she had not moved, he looked up. 'Well, why are you standing there on one leg? Practising to be a stork?'

She ignored the sarcasm. 'Dinner will be served in the breakfast-room at eight o'clock, sir. There's roast beef and Yorkshire pudding.'

'You know what you can do with it,' he said in the gentlest of tones.

Red-cheeked, Anthea stood her ground and pretended to misunderstand him. 'I don't enjoy eating roast beef on my own, sir.'

He pushed at his spectacles. 'Is that an invitation, Miss

Wilmot?'

Too late she realised he had misinterpreted her words. 'Of course not, sir.'

'What a pity! The rare presence of your company might have gone well with the rare roast beef! But as you don't wish me to dine with you. . . .' He lowered his head to his papers. 'Just sandwiches, please, Miss Wilmot.'

The tiredness in his voice was her undoing. 'I'm quite willing to have dinner with you, sir.'

'Are you?' He looked up again. 'A great concession made to save your employer from dying of an overdose of sandwiches!'

'We all enjoy working for you, sir. If you died on us, we would have to find other employment.'

He laughed outright, and dropping his pen on to his desk, leaned back in his chair and stretched. 'I'm exhausted. It will probably do me good to have a break for a few hours. I'll see you in the dining-room at eight.'

'Very good, sir.' She was at the door when he called after her:

'Better make it seven-thirty in the drawing-room. Then we can have a drink.'

Inordinately pleased at the suggestion, Anthea almost skipped upstairs to her room, and promptly to time was down in the hall again, hovering outside the drawing-room door until the chiming of a distant grandfather clock gave her the impetus to go in.

Her employer was already there, elegant in black velvet trousers and dark green velvet jacket. For a conservative businessman he had a stylish wardrobe, and she wondered what he wore when he was in London. Velvet suited his looks, the sheen of the material echoing the sheen of his jet black hair, and his white silk shirt emphasised his bronze skin. There was foreign blood in him somewhere, she decided, and was intrigued to know more of his background.

He did not ask her what she would like to drink, but handed her a silver goblet whose interior effervesced with champagne.

'I hope you drink champagne, Miss Wilmot?'

She sipped appreciatively. 'It makes a change from bitter lemon, sir.'

'Come now, don't tell me you can't drink champagne if you want to? There are cases of it in the wine cellar.'

Her head tilted sharply. 'None of the staff touch your wines or spirits, Mr. Allen.'

'Sorry,' he said quickly, 'it was just my little joke.' He perched on the arm of a chair and idly swung one leg. 'Seriously though, there's no reason why you can't open a bottle of wine if you want. Champagne too, for that matter. I'm perfectly happy for you to have the entire run of my home and its contents.'

She acknowledged the offer with a slight smile, but made no comment on it. He too seemed content to be silent, humming softly as he drank his champagne and then replenished both their goblets.

Leggat entered to announce dinner, and they followed him into the small dining-room.

'I understand Jackson Pollard was here yesterday?' Mark Allen said as they began to eat. 'What did you think of him?'

'I liked him. I didn't think I would.'

'Claudine's a good judge of decorators. She's had more practice than any woman I know.'

'She does it professionally, then?'

He shook his head. 'She re-does her house whenever the mood takes her—which is every year or so—and she's always changing the odd room around.'

'How strange. I like my home to be familiar—and it can't, if you keep altering things.'

'I agree.' He signalled Leggat to leave them alone, saying

he would pour the wine himself and ring if he needed anything. 'I have the feeling you're on the defensive when Leggat is around,' he remarked as the door closed behind the butler.

'Surely that's understandable? After all, I didn't get the impression from Mrs. Goodbody that you dined with *her* all that often!'

'Never,' he grinned. 'And if you were like dear Mrs. Goodbody, you'd be on the never list too!'

'I didn't realise I was so different.'

'You're younger.' He smiled and leaned forward. 'You shouldn't wear such pale powder, Miss Wilmot. In fact you don't need powder at all. You have an excellent skin.'

She concentrated on cutting her beef.

'Now I've embarrassed you,' he said. 'I'm sorry. I didn't mean to do so.'

It was too genuine an apology for her to ignore, and she gave him a beaming smile which elicited another penetrating glance from him. But he made no personal remarks and they chatted desultorily until the meal was over and they returned to the drawing-room for coffee.

At ten o'clock he stood up reluctantly. 'I must get on with my work, I'm afraid. I have a meeting with Jasper Goderick in the morning.'

'So you won't be here for the rest of the weekend?' She could not keep the disappointment from her voice, but he did not seem to be aware of it, his mind already back in the library among his papers.

'Thank you for sharing my dinner, Miss Wilmot. I'll see you some time during the week.'

He left in the morning without saying goodbye to her. There was no reason why he should have done, and she was angry for being disappointed. If she had known he was going to leave on Sunday she would have arranged to see Roger. She looked at the telephone, debating whether or not to call him, and then decided against it. Instead she went home.

Only as Chrissy opened the door, her face looking first delighted and then upset, did Anthea discover that her father and stepmother had gone to the coast for the week-end.

'Mrs. Wilmot thought the sea air would do your father good,' Chrissy sniffed.

'It probably will,' Anthea said cheerily. 'Don't be so prejudiced!'

'She takes a bit of getting used to,' Chrissy said lugubriously, 'but she's better than I expected.'

'And my father is happy?' Anthea pressed home the point.

'Yes, he is,' the housekeeper agreed. 'Mrs Wilmot dotes on him and he enjoys it.'

'All men enjoy having women dote on them.' As Anthea spoke a picture of Claudine came into her mind. It refused to fade and marred her pleasure at being back among her own possessions and able to wear her normal clothes.

Was Mark Allen seeing Jasper Goderick alone this afternoon or was the beautiful Frenchwoman with them? She would have given a great deal to know the answer, and because there was no likelihood of her doing so, she telephoned Roger. An evening with him would make her forget her intriguing employer.

'How many girl-friends are sitting on your lap?' she asked as he answered.

'I'm as free as a bird,' he said promptly.

'Will you promise not to turn into a wolf if I go out with you this evening?'

'Try me,' he whooped. 'I'll be round pronto!'

He was as good as his word, and Anthea felt her spirits lift as she sat beside him in his open sports car and roared down the road an hour later. It was good to be herself again; to say what she wanted without having to monitor it and to refer to her past and future without feeling she was giving herself away. Not having to censor her thoughts, she was more relaxed and affectionate than she realised, a fact which he took advantage of when he finally brought her home, for he pulled her into his arms and began to kiss her passionately.

She suffered his touch for a moment, but as his kisses intensified, she pushed him away. 'No, Roger. Please don't.'

'What's wrong?' he asked.

'You're a bird, remember? Not a wolf.'

'At least let me be a cub?' He went to pull her close again, but she evaded him and jumped out of the car.

'Three o'clock tomorrow,' he called. 'That's the time we arranged.'

Unable to face seeing him again so soon, she lied, 'I can't make it, I'm afraid. I thought you realised that when I saw you today instead?'

He looked so disconsolate that she almost changed her mind, but knowing she would regret it in the morning if she did, she remained silent.

'What about next weekend?' he asked.

'Let me phone you. I never know when I'm going to be free.'

'That Allen certainly keeps your nose to the grindstone,' he grumbled. 'Doesn't he know Abraham Lincoln abolished slavery?'

'I'm a willing slave,' she smiled, and sidestepped him as his arms came out to catch her. 'Goodnight, Roger.'

'What's good about it?' he grumbled.

'I'm good!' she laughed, and closed the door before he could think up a suitable reply.

Lying in her bed staring at the pink roses climbing the walls, she found she was homesick for her bedroom at Bar-

93

tham Manor. Yet it was not the house itself which drew her back but the fact that when she was in it she felt closer to its owner. It was a sobering thought and conjured up other more frightening ones. Resolutely she pushed them away and thought instead of October.

In another six weeks Betsy would be ready to start work and she herself would be free. But she was not going to come back here. She would go to London and try to get another temporary job as a housekeeper. There was a lot to be said for a position that gave her room and board and sufficient free time to continue her studies. Of course a job like her present one would not be easy to find, but she was sure she could obtain one that was nearly as good. It might be better to find a woman employer instead of a man. They could be more difficult, it was true, but it was less likely to give her any emotional problems.

Once more her thoughts had come full circle, and agitated at where they had led her, she sat up in bed. It was stupid of her to continue thinking of Mark Allen. As far as he was concerned she was someone who looked after his country house; someone with whom he could while away a few tedious hours. When he was in London he probably never even gave her a thought. Sobered by this knowledge, she settled back on her pillow, though it was a long time before she finally fell asleep.

Anthea waited at home until mid-afternoon the following day in the hope of seeing her father, but when three o'clock came and went she was reluctantly forced to leave. Chrissy had gone out shopping and she was able to braid her hair and put on her dowdy dress in safety.

As she rode along the country lanes she felt her spirits lift. It was another lovely day with the temperature well in the high sixties. What a pity there was no swimming pool at Bartham Manor. She was surprised Mark Allen had not put one in.

The wrought iron gates of his home loomed ahead of her and she signalled the conductor to stop the bus, then ambled leisurely up the drive.

As she came in sight of the Manor she stopped with a gasp. Her father's car was parked by the side of a flowering acacia. He and Maude must have come to see her.

Heart pounding, she sped through the courtyard to the back of the house, and it was here that she received her second shock. Mark Allen's Rolls gleamed darkly in the garage. Oh no! That was all she needed.

The urge to turn tail and run was so strong that it required all her will power not to give in to it. Instead she raced indoors in search of Leggat.

He was polishing some silver in the butler's pantry and he looked up at her precipitate entry and spoke before she had a chance to do so herself. 'Your parents are here, Miss Wilmot. I've just served them tea in the rose arbour.'

Nodding her thanks, she hurried out and across the lawn. Long before she reached the arbour she heard her stepmother's booming voice and slackened her step.

'Anthea made us promise not to come and see her without telephoning first,' Maude was saying, 'but the Professor and I were passing and it seemed silly not to call in.'

'I'm glad you did,' a quiet voice said, and Anthea gave a shiver of apprehension. Mark Allen couldn't be talking to her stepmother. But he was, and very pleasant he sounded too, as he went into a discourse on roses.

'I am extremely fond of gardening,' Maude Wilmot told him. 'But unfortunately Anthea and my husband aren't. They are great ones for picking but not for growing!'

'Miss Wilmot is excellent at arranging flowers,' Anthea heard her employer say.

'Better than her typing, I should think,' Professor Wilmot chuckled. 'How are you finding that?'

'Your daughter has not done any typing for me.'

'Surely you can't correct your notes from a dictaphone? I thought Anthea was typing them back?'

'I think Anthea is doing research, dear,' Maude put in. 'That may not require typing.'

'Your daughter definitely doesn't do any typing for me,' Mark Allen repeated. 'I certainly wouldn't expect her to be my secretary as well.'

'As well as what?' asked Maude ominously.

'As well as being my housekeeper.'

'*Your* housekeeper?' The shocked tones reminded Anthea of Dame Edith Evans as Lady Bracknell; and she waited for her stepmother to say: '*A handbag?*'

But when Mrs. Wilmot spoke, it was only to repeat her original words: 'Your *housekeeper?*'

'Yes,' said Mark Allen. 'And an excellent one, I'm delighted to say.'

'Frederick!' said his wife. 'Did you hear that?'

'I did indeed.' Professor Wilmot's voice was mildly amused and Anthea could almost see the twinkle in his eyes. 'It seems my daughter is involved in a little charade. She informed us that she was here as your research assistant.'

'She is standing in for a friend of hers, who is ill,' Mark Allen replied. 'A Miss Betsy Evans. I understood they are friends.'

There was a short silence, broken finally by Professor Wilmot who murmured that his daughter must be referring to Betsy Evans, a friend of his housekeeper.

'It's just the sort of thing Anthea would do,' he added. 'But kind of her, don't you think?'

'Frederick is so *right*.' Maude gushed back into the conversation, making the best of a situation she neither liked nor comprehended. 'Anthea is such an impulsive girl, you know. But then young people are like that these days, and Anthea is more impulsive than most.'

FOUR BEST SELLER ROMANCES FREE

Best Seller Romance — **Mills & Boon** — Best Seller Romance — **Mills & Boon** — Best Seller Romance — **Mills & Boon** — Best

FORBIDDEN RAPTURE
Violet Winspear

TEMPORARY WIFE
Roberta Leigh

THE BENEDICT MAN
Mary Wibberley

MA OF TH
Lilia

Enjoy the books that have enthralled hundreds of readers

Turn the page for details of this exciting offer

'I wouldn't have said so,' Mark Allen replied. 'She's always struck me as being eminently practical and serious.'

'She's very lively and extrovert,' Mrs. Wilmot insisted. 'And so lovely. The young men just flock round her!'

'Really?' Anthea squirmed at the disbelief in her employer's voice.

'Indeed they do,' her stepmother continued. 'But she has no time for a serious romance. She wants to get her degree first.'

'Very sensible too,' Professor Wilmot added. 'Marriage can always come afterwards.'

'Your daughter is probably wise to concentrate on a career,' Mark Allen said.

'She won't be allowed to concentrate on it for long.' Maude Wilmot was nothing if not persistent. 'She's far too beautiful to become a blue-stocking. Don't you think so, Mr. Allen?'

'Beauty is relative,' came the cool response.

'But Anthea is *so* striking. Everyone says so. She'll make a wonderful wife. Beauty and brains rarely go together, I find. I'm sure you agree with me, Mr. Allen. That's probably why you are still unmarried.'

'I happen to prefer my freedom.' The words were sharp but not sharp enough to penetrate Maude's thick skin.

'Stronger men than you have succumbed to my stepdaughter's charm,' she said archly. 'Does Anthea act as your hostess? It would be such a pity if she didn't.'

'My aunt normally does that. I never use my housekeeper.'

Unable to bear any more, Anthea braced her shoulders and stepped into the rose garden.

'Hello,' she said brightly, and fixed her eyes on her father.

'My dear,' he murmured. 'How lovely to see you.'

'Why are you dressed like that?' Mrs. Wilmot asked.

'And what on earth have you done to your hair?'

Only then did Anthea remember her unbecoming black dress and ridiculous plait. 'I like to keep it out of my eyes,' she mumbled, and moving over to the tray on the wrought-iron table picked up the teapot.

'Your parents assumed you were my secretary,' a quiet voice said beside her.

'It was a slight misunderstanding.' Anthea could not keep the tremor out of her voice as she went on pouring the tea.

'Very slight,' he said.

Ignoring the comment, Anthea passed the tea to her father and stepmother. 'Will you have a cup, Mr. Allen?' she asked, still not looking at him.

'No, thank you. But do have one yourself.'

'I'm not thirsty.' The thought of trying to swallow tea was impossible. She glanced at her father and saw him looking at her with the bland expression he usually wore when he was trying to hide his amusement.

'Why didn't you let me know you were coming?' she asked.

'Maude wanted to surprise you.'

'She's certainly done that,' said Mark Allen. 'She has surprised us both.' He glanced at Mrs. Wilmot. 'But I'm delighted you and your husband have paid me a visit. Now if you'll excuse me, I have work to do.'

'Of course,' the good lady replied. 'I do hope you'll come and visit *us* one day.'

'I'm sure Mr. Allen has more to do with his time than spend it with an elderly professor and his wife,' her husband said.

'Not when the professor is Frederick Wilmot,' came the instant reply. 'I'm a great admirer of your work. I particularly enjoyed your last book.'

'How kind of you to say so.'

Anthea remained staring down at the grass, and a pair of

98

shiny leather shoes came within her vision. 'When your parents have gone, Miss Wilmot, perhaps you would come and see me in the library.'

'Yes, Mr. Allen,' she said, and did not raise her eyes until she heard his steps recede across the flagstone path.

CHAPTER EIGHT

WITH trepidation Anthea went in search of Mark Allen as soon as her father and stepmother had left. The hour she had spent with them had been a difficult one, not so much because of what they had said to her but because of what they had left unsaid. She had overheard enough of Maude's conversation with her employer to know that he must realise that her appearance was a fraud and that she had lied to her parents regarding the work she was doing for him. She could not blame him for being very angry about it and hoped he had sufficient sense of humour to see the funny side of the situation.

One look at his face as she went into the library told her he was not amused at all. Indeed she had never seen him more angry, though it was a controlled anger which seemed to come from deep within him; a fact confirmed by his opening remark.

'You're exactly like the rest of your sex—out to get what you want—and you don't give a tinker's cuss how you do it!'

'There was no ulterior motive in what I did, Mr. Allen.'

'Do you expect me to believe that?'

'It's true.'

'You came here to act as my housekeeper; you dressed up like something out of a Victorian orphanage! You told your parents you were my secretary and that I was an old man, and you expect me to believe you had no ulterior motive? My God, Miss Wilmot, I'd more easily swallow a whale than that lot!'

'I don't see why you should be so annoyed,' she murmured. 'After all, I haven't done anything criminal.'

'You don't think it was wrong to come here under false pretences?'

'They weren't false pretences. I came here to save the job for Miss Evans. That's perfectly valid. The only thing that—the only way I pretended was by trying to make myself look older.'

'As well as uglier and more stupid!' he spat out.

'I don't think you ever believed me to be stupid,' she said quietly.

He paused momentarily. 'That's true. I found you surprisingly intelligent and—— But I appear to have underestimated even that. You are not only intelligent but enterprising. It was a stroke of genius to insinuate yourself into my life the way you did. To pretend you didn't care about clothes and the way you looked; to encourage me to relax with you and to be off my guard. When I think of it I could....' He banged his hand on the desk and swung round to face the window, as if he could not bear the sight of her.

Anthea stared at his back in astonishment. Only now did she begin to understand why he was so bitter. His anger was not directed against her so much as all the other women he had known; women who had pretended to be what they were not in order to penetrate his guard. The sort of women who had seen him as a bank balance and not as a man. But surely he didn't believe she had adopted a disguise for the same reason? The thought made her hot with embarrassment, the more so as she realised that in the last few weeks she had seen him far less as a financier who lived in the rarefied atmosphere of city life, and more as a young man with too much responsibility; a man made old before his time by the mantle of success which he wore so well in public but which weighed so heavily on him in private.

'I didn't come here for any ulterior motive,' she said firmly. 'The only reason I made myself look older and—and—and different was because I was afraid you wouldn't accept me in Miss Evans's place if I looked too young. Besides, I had to impress Mrs. Goodbody, and she'd never have taken me if she'd known my age.'

He swung back to look at her. 'How old are you?'

Anthea hesitated.

'The truth, Miss Wilmot.'

She swallowed. 'Twenty-two.'

'Twenty-two! You're damn right she wouldn't have taken you! Any more than I'll take you. . . . I'd like you to pack your things and leave. Herbert will drive you to your home.'

She looked at him in bewilderment. This was something she had never envisaged. 'Why are you dismissing me? I know I've satisfied you as a housekeeper and——'

'That has nothing to do with it. You came here under false pretences and I have no intention of allowing you to remain.' He sat down at his desk and pulled some papers towards him, indicating that the interview was over.

But Anthea had no intention of being dismissed so easily, and she advanced towards him, guilt at her subterfuge giving way to temper at his attitude.

'How can you be so unfeeling!' she cried. 'If you were displeased with me I could understand you asking me to leave. But why does it matter what I look like or how old I am, so long as I do my job to your satisfaction?'

'You came here because you wanted to inveigle yourself into my life. It was a clever scheme, Miss Wilmot, I grant you that, but unfortunately it hasn't worked.'

Once again she was speechless; then the full flood of her

fury washed away the last vestige of reserve. 'If you think I came here because I wanted to get to know you, you must be out of your mind! I'd never heard of you until Betsy mentioned your name. To me, you're no more real than the gnomes of Switzerland and just about as important in my life! You may be considered a catch by the world's socialites, but as far as I'm concerned, Mr. Allen, you're a dreary man who wastes his life making money! If you think I'd go to the bother of wearing these stupid clothes and making myself miserable every time I look in the mirror, just to get to know *you....*'

Words failed her and she turned round and marched to the door. But the thought of Betsy made her stop and turn again.

'I think it would be monstrously unfair of you not to keep the job open for Miss Evans. Your home has been perfectly run while I've been here, and your staff have had no complaints to make about me. If you insist on my leaving tonight, at least have the decency to—to——' She swallowed hard and began again. 'Betsy will be well enough to come here in a month. I'm sure Mr. and Mrs. Leggat can manage everything here until then.'

'Your concern for your friend does you credit,' he said sarcastically, 'but I'd appreciate it if you would allow me to run my home the way I see fit.'

'But Mrs. Leggat can——'

'Only cope if I don't do any entertaining. She has no sense of detail. Had it not been for that, I would never have tried to find a replacement for Mrs. Goodbody. But the moment there's a change in routine, Mrs. Leggat gets flustered. I'll be giving several weekend parties this coming month and she'll never be able to manage.'

With a sigh Anthea went towards the door. Pleading was a waste of time; she might as well accept the inevitable and leave. What a beast the man was! Tears welled into her eyes and she blinked them away, so intent on getting out before he could see how upset she was that she did not hear him call her until he repeated her name loudly.

'What do you want?' she whispered, keeping her face averted.

'I said that as you seem so concerned for Miss Evans, I have decided to let you stay. Not because I condone your behaviour but because I appreciate why you did it.'

She turned to him at once, her eyes alight with pleasure. 'I'm so glad, Mr. Allen. And believe me, I didn't come here because I wanted to meet you.'

'You've made that quite clear. I hadn't realised you regarded my work with such disfavour.'

She flushed. 'I shouldn't have spoken to you like that. I'm sorry.'

His laugh was sharp and brief. 'Don't apologise for honesty. It's a rare quality and I appreciate it.'

'I really did think you were old,' she said impulsively. 'When Mrs. Goodbody spoke about you, she gave the impression that you were——'

'You needn't bother with any more explanations,' he said coldly, and fingered some papers on his desk. 'But for the rest of your time here, it will irritate me far less if you revert to your normal mode of dress and behaviour.'

'Behaviour?' She was puzzled. 'I can dress normally, of course, but I could never *act* normally with you.'

'Why not?'

'I might be too frank.'

His lower lip jutted forward, and above the heavy rims of his spectacles his eyebrows met in a frown. 'I would prefer your frankness to a continuance of your charade.'

'Very well, Mr. Allen. I'll do as you say.'

This time he did not call her back, and she went out of the library and up to her room. Her pleasure in being able to look and dress normally was lessened by her fear of Mark

103

Allen's reaction to it. Still, even if he did not like her looking young and presentable, he had agreed to let her remain until Betsy was able to take over, and he was not likely to go back on his word.

To her disappointment she did not see him again that evening, for he had supper served on a tray in the library and left for London early the following morning.

But the change in her appearance did not go unremarked by the rest of the staff, who treated her with greater friendliness though the same amount of respect. Mrs. Leggat became considerably more motherly, and the young maids—foreign girls anxious to earn money while they learned English—treated her as their confidante.

Unregretfully Anthea bundled up her two plain dresses and the hideous flowered one and marched with them to the village, where she deposited them with the vicar's wife who was collecting old clothes for the Church bazaar.

'My dear child,' that good lady said when Anthea introduced herself as Mark Allen's housekeeper, 'what an unusual occupation for someone of your age!'

'It's ideal,' Anthea smiled. 'How else could I get to live in such a beautiful house?'

'How else indeed.' The grey eyes were slightly sharp as they rested on Anthea's rounded limbs and short cotton dress.

The lengthening of sunlight had given her a delicate tan, while the tranquil hours and early nights gave a noticeable bloom to her appearance. Eventually she knew she would become bored by this placid existence, but for the moment she was enjoying it and, with her books to study, she did not find the evenings lonely. But seeing the vicar's wife eyeing her, she could appreciate why her employer preferred to have an elderly housekeeper.

'I'm only standing in for my friend, Miss Evans,' she explained, thinking it best to set the record straight, and knowing that by doing it this way she could be sure of everyone in the village hearing about it. 'I'm going back to university in October.'

Mention of a university had the expected effect, and despising herself for it, though none the less considering it necessary, Anthea also casually referred to her father. There was nothing like throwing in a professor for good measure.

'My dear,' the vicar's wife exclaimed, 'you must come to tea and meet my husband. He's devoted to history and spends all his time searching out the history of the parishioners here. Such fascinating lives some of them had, and much more imaginative and busy when they were forced to make the village the centre of their world. Now that London is so easy to get to on the motorway, it's becoming like a suburb here.'

Confident of having restored her own good name, as well as maintaining that of Mark Allen's, Anthea returned to Bartham Manor. Jackson Pollard's car was parked in the drive and she went into the main hall in search of him.

He was in the dining-room measuring the table, and he glanced at her briefly and then continued with his perusal.

'I didn't know you were coming down today, Mr. Pollard,' she said. 'I would appreciate it if you would telephone me next time and let me know.'

'Telephone *you*?' His quizzical look suddenly disappeared. 'Good gracious! If it hadn't been for your voice, I would never have recognized you. What have you done to yourself?'

'Summer clothes,' she said briefly.

'A great improvement on your winter ones.' His blond eyebrows rose and lowered. 'I came down to check on some more measurements and because Mrs. Goderick wanted to see some of the materials in situ. Colours have a habit of looking different when in different environments. It's a question of light and space, I suppose.'

'I'm sure Miss Wilmot doesn't want to be bothered with the secrets of your profession, Jackson,' came a lilting voice with a faint French-Canadian accent.

Anthea turned as Claudine Goderick came in. She braced herself for the woman's surprise, but was unprepared for her anger which, though quickly masked, was too unmistakable to be misinterpreted. But Claudine made no comment on Anthea's change of dress and make-up, and immediately began to talk to the interior decorator about the refurnishing of the hall.

'The panelling must be stripped,' she ordered, 'and the original colouring of the woodwork restored. Then a dark red stair carpet and Persian runners on the floor.'

'Excellent,' the man said. 'What do you feel about the drawing-room?'

'Let's take the swatches of material you've suggested and hold them up against the settees.'

Ignoring Anthea, Claudine went into the drawing-room. Her high heels clattered on the parquet floor and she moved with sinuous grace. Even without her husband's doting glance and Mark Allen's admiring one, she still exuded the air of a self-satisfied cat.

Although there was no reason for Anthea to remain with the visitors, something impelled her to do so, and she went with them from room to room, listening as decisions were made regarding furniture and curtains, carpets and wall-paper. The various samples of fabrics were held up for Claudine Goderick's inspection, and Anthea saw that the woman's taste veered towards the exotic rather than the rustic, which she personally felt would have been more suitable to a country mansion. Bartham Manor was not a home which called for chintz and pewter, but neither was it right for satin and velvet. She was disappointed that Mark Allen was satisfied to leave all the decisions to

Claudine. Surely he could have found a few hours to spare to give *some* thought to all the changes being planned. After all, it was his home and he lived here; not a hotel.

With a start she realised Claudine Goderick was speaking to her, her voice irritable as she repeated her question.

'I asked you what you thought of the colour schemes I've chosen for the Manor.'

'They seem fine,' Anthea lied. 'Though I didn't pay all that much attention to them. Decorating a house is like preparing a dinner party. Too many cooks spoil the broth!'

'How tactful you are!' Jackson Pollard chuckled.

'Tact is a quality Mr. Allen looks for in all his employees,' Claudine said, and gave Anthea a cold glance. 'I'll no doubt be seeing you at the weekend. My husband and I are coming down.'

'I hope the good weather holds,' Anthea replied pleasantly.

'The company interests me more than the weather,' Claudine smiled, and went down the steps to Jackson Pollard's car.

As soon as it had disappeared down the drive, Anthea closed and locked the front door. It was silly to let Claudine irritate her. In a few weeks her stint as a housekeeper would be over and she would never see the woman again. Nor Mark Allen either. Somehow she knew it was not going to be easy to forget either the house or its owner, for in their own way they had each made an indelible impression on her; the house for its beautiful setting and elegantly proportioned rooms; the owner for his quick mind and unpredictable moods.

Quickly she walked across the hall to the servants' quarters and closed the communicating door, as if in so doing she could shut out the thoughts that were disturbing her.

CHAPTER NINE

As she had anticipated, Anthea received a call from Mark Allen's secretary telling her he would be having a weekend house-party and requesting her to prepare all the guest rooms. This meant that at least twelve people would be coming, and she was not surprised when Monsieur Marcel arrived on Thursday evening instead of Friday and immediately set to work in the kitchen.

Happily he treated Mrs. Leggat as his equal, accepting her offer to prepare some of the dishes and discussing with her the menus he planned to serve for the three days.

The house-party was to begin with dinner on Friday and would continue until Sunday evening, most of the guests departing before supper, and the rest immediately afterwards. Armed with a list of names, Anthea consulted the guest book and noted the idiosyncrasies of all those she could find listed there; then she allocated them to their rooms, remembering to give the Godericks the suite they always occupied.

For the whole of Friday morning she was busy filling the house with flowers; not the potted plants her employer liked, but large, casual bouquets of country flowers which were her own particular favourites. It was amazing what a transformation these made to the overpowering furnishings, and she could not stifle a pang of regret that she would not be able to see the house when it had been redecorated. Even if she did not agree with all that was going to be done, it would be a great improvement on the present.

Early in the afternoon she went into town to collect the new uniforms for the maids. She had ordered them on her own initiative, finding that the black dresses and white aprons which the girls wore in the evening were too reminiscent of waitresses. Instead she had chosen dark blue nylon overalls for them to wear during the day and coffee-brown dresses for them to change into from lunchtime onwards. It was a colour that would suit most types of skin, and the simple style of plain bodice and gently eased skirt was one which Anthea would have been happy to wear herself. Only when she paid the bill—which seemed inordinately large— did she have a qualm of fear at not having agreed the expenditure with her employer first. But taken singly the dresses were inexpensive: it was only in total that the amount seemed so large. But it was too late to do anything about it except pay, and armed with the dress boxes she returned to the Manor.

The grey Rolls was already in the drive, and seeing it she quickly cut off across the lawn and headed for the side entrance. Her heart raced and she experienced an odd sense of excitement which not even logic could dispel. If she had used her sense she would have foreseen that with such a large house-party, Mark Allen was bound to come home earlier than usual to check for himself that everything was in order. Particularly since he now knew her real age and had made no secret of the fact that he considered her too young for her job. Hard on this recollection came the reminder that today he would be seeing her without her disguise. Her heart raced faster still, and her mouth was so dry that when she gave the dress boxes to Elsie—with instructions for the maids to change at once—she had to moisten her lips before she could speak.

Then she raced up to her bedroom. The desire to put on something long and black was so strong that she was glad she had given her dresses to the vicar's wife; again she was disconcerted by her embarrassment, and refusing to clarify it, concentrated on making herself presentable. She put on a fresh linen dress whose creamy colour made her hair look tawny, and applied lipstick and mascara. They made her long ashes look theatrically false, but there was no time for her to wash it off. She'd just have to remember not to blink them at Mark Allen!

Keeping her lids lowered, she hurried back to her sitting-room, entering it the same moment that the bell rang from the library. Chin up, Anthea went to answer it.

Outside the library she stopped. Her hands were clammy, but she resisted the urge to wipe them on her dress and, giving a peremptory knock on the door, went in.

Her employer was standing by the window with his back to the light, so she could not see his expression. But she knew he was watching her as she came to stand by his desk: a tall, slim girl with the lithe grace of youth and the confident ease of someone who knew they were good to look upon. She tilted her head and the thick brown hair rippled round her shoulders.

'You wanted to see me, Mr. Allen?'

'Only to talk about the arrangements for the weekend.' His voice was staccato, as if he were talking to a stranger.

'I've prepared a list of the bedrooms allocated to each guest.' She handed him a sheet of paper and he took it and dropped it on his desk without glancing at it.

'I'm sure you've arranged everything perfectly, Miss Wilmot. Spare me further proof of your ability.'

'You said you wish to discuss the arrangements, sir. I thought you would consider *that* to be one of them.'

There was silence and Anthea waited for his wrath to explode. Instead he shrugged and sat down at his desk. She could see his face clearly now, and was surprised by his pallor, which gave his tan a yellowish tinge. There was unaccustomed stubble on his jawline, as though he had not shaved close enough that morning. Or perhaps his morning had begun earlier than usual: at some ungodly hour when he should—by rights—have still been sleeping.

110

'You look tired,' she said impulsively.

'I am. I've had an extremely busy week.'

'I'll bring you some tea.'

'Don't bother.'

'It's no bother, sir. Dinner isn't till eight-thirty, and that's a long time ahead.'

His only answer was another shrug, and Anthea went to the kitchen and made some sandwiches and a pot of tea herself, telling Leggat—who was busy supervising the final polishing of the silver—that she would serve it too. Carrying the tray, together with some freshly cut sandwiches, she returned to the library.

There was no answer to her knock and wondering if he had heard it, she went in. He was sitting at his desk and she had reached it before she realised he was asleep. Softly she set the tray down. She was reluctant to wake him, yet knew that if she did not do so the tea would grow cold. She leaned forward and then stopped. In repose he looked even more tired, though oddly he appeared younger. Perhaps it was because he was no longer controlling his expression. His mouth, normally firmly closed, had relaxed into unexpectedly soft lines, the top lip delicately curved, the lower one full and sensuous. His chin was no longer fierce either, and his cheeks—slack with sleep—seemed boyishly young, as did the two half circles of black lashes that edged the blue shadowed lids.

Suddenly Anthea realised she was seeing him without his glasses. They lay on the blotter in front of him, as though they had been carelessly discarded. Idly she picked them up. How heavy they were! No wonder they left a mark across his nose. It was a nice nose now that she could see it properly: firm and straight with narrow flaring nostrils. She lifted up his glasses and stared through them. Everything was distorted; the objects around her blurred and diminished in size. She set the glasses down but remained

111

looking at him, seeing a streak of grey in the jet black hair. It was silky hair and looked as it it would be soft to the touch. His eyelids fluttered and unexpectedly lifted and Anthea found herself staring directly into dark grey irises. She had never seen his eyes without their lenses and she was astonished by their vulnerability. They were the eyes of a child: large and myopic, shiny and clear. Then the lids came down swiftly and he reached out for his spectacles and put them firmly on his nose.

'What do you want?' he demanded. He saw the tray on the desk before she could answer, and gave a grunt. 'I didn't ask for sandwiches.'

'It's your own home-cured ham, sir. You're hardly ever here to taste it.'

'Stop mothering me, Miss Wilmot.'

She flushed at the sarcasm, embarrassed because she knew she had deserved it. 'I'm sorry, sir.'

'For God's sake stop sirring me all the time!'

'Yes, Mr. Allen.'

'And don't Mr. Allen me either!'

She hid a smile. He was as irritable as small boys often were when awoken from sleep.

'What's the joke?' he asked.

Knowing he would not appreciate it, she shook her head and went to pour him his tea.

'Leave it,' he ordered. 'I'm not helpless.' He sighed. 'Oh, very well, you might as well pour since you're standing there.' She did so and set it before him, together with the sandwiches which he began to eat abstractedly.

'Will that be all?' she asked.

'Yes, thank you.'

Anthea hesitated, undecided whether to tell him about the new uniforms she had bought for the maids. To do so might bring forth another burst of temper about being bothered with unimportant details, but not to do so could equally annoy him, especially if he was presented with the bill at a time when he was irritable.

'Well, Miss Wilmot, what mischief have you been up to this time?'

Annoyed at the implication that she had been doing something wrong, her eyes sparkled angrily. 'My behaviour here has always been exemplary. I was merely wondering whether or not to bother you with the trivialities of the household.'

'The fact that you're worried whether you should do so or not leads me to believe you *don't* consider it such a triviality.'

'I bought new uniforms for the maids,' she blurted out. 'I was going to check with you first, but it didn't seem worth-while. They were only a few pounds each.'

'Then what's the problem?'

'I ordered two dresses for each maid and the bill came to more than I realised.'

'I fail to see why,' he said blandly. 'To arrive at the sum total only means simple multiplication.'

'I didn't do the multiplication until I had to pay. That's when I realised it was a larger sum than I'd thought.'

'How much?'

'Sixty pounds.'

'That's rather a lot for you to spend without authority. Of course,' he added, 'I can always deduct it from your salary.'

Her head lifted sharply, but just in time she saw the glint in his eyes and knew he was deliberately trying to provoke her.

'As your housekeeper, I'm supposed to have carte blanche in the running of your home.'

'Carte blanche within reason.'

'Sixty pounds is not unreasonable for a man in your position.'

'Don't use my position as an excuse for extravagance. Either the amount is reasonable or it isn't.'

'One can't ignore your position. What's reasonable for you is not reasonable for a farmhand.'

His sigh was mildly exasperated but gave indication that his tiredness was still with him.

'Drink your tea and have a rest,' Anthea said before she could stop herself. 'I'll come in and wake you up at six.'

'If I decide to have a rest, Miss Wilmot, I can also arrange to have myself woken up without enlisting your aid.'

'Yes, Mr. Allen. I'll remember not to offer my services in future—sir!' she added, and closed the door quickly behind her before he could reply.

Irrationally hurt by his sharp response to her solicitude over his tiredness, she tried to adopt her normal policy of pushing him out of her mind. But she was not successful and he remained disturbingly vivid.

By seven that evening all the guests had arrived, and at eight-thirty dinner was served in the main dining-room. Supervising the final laying of the table and setting out the place cards to follow the list sent to her by Mark Allen's secretary, Anthea noted with something akin to irritation that Claudine Goderick was placed on his right—as she was for every meal. Was this because he was in the middle of business negotiations with the woman's husband or because he genuinely liked her and wished to have her beside him?

From Claudine's general air as she had wandered around Bartham Manor with Jackson Pollard earlier in the week, Anthea was convinced it was the latter reason; was convinced too that Claudine returned the interest. Not because she needed Mark Allen among her possessions—with a husband like Jasper Goderick she already had all the possessions an acquisitive woman could require—but because Mark Allen appealed to her as a man. It was amazing that

114

he had managed to escape the snare of matrimony for so long, and she wondered if it was because he was too involved with work to fall in love or because the woman he loved was not available.

This brought her back to Claudine, and she watched the woman during Friday evening and Saturday, aware of how firmly she attached herself to her host, regardless of her husband watching her possessively, bitterly and yet at the same time triumphantly—as if he knew that, come what may, she belonged only to him; a property he had bought and had no intention of relinquishing.

Leggat too noticed Claudine Goderick's possessive attitude towards his employer and, unexpectedly for him, for he was the soul of discretion, commented on it as he and his wife joined Anthea and Monsieur Marcel for a late supper.

'She even keeps a notebook by the side of her plate,' he commented. 'And I've noticed her jotting things down in it. You'd think she was the mistress here already.'

'She may well be Mr. Allen's mistress,' Monsieur Marcel smiled.

'That wasn't what I meant,' the butler said hastily.

'I know what you meant, my good friend,' the chef chuckled. 'But when a woman like Mrs. Goderick knows she is desired by a man, she immediately tries to make herself indispensable to him—in every way.'

'You're right there,' Leggat replied, and looked at Anthea. 'Mark my words, she'll be calling you in to see her before she leaves and giving you her opinion about the weekend. She isn't making those notes for her own amusement.'

'She'd better not make any criticisms direct to me,' Anthea said firmly. 'I work for Mr. Allen; no one else.' The three people in the room looked at each other and Anthea said defiantly: 'I mean it. I won't be ordered around by Claudine Goderick.'

'If she calls you,' Monsieur Marcel murmured, 'I would like very much to be a fly on the wall!'

Anthea smiled and helped herself to some more of the chef's delicious pâté. But not even the excellent food nor the wine which Mark Allen had thoughtfully arranged for them to have could still the red-hot anger that the butler's words had aroused. What sort of man was Mark Allen to allow a stranger to criticise the running of his home? If he wished to accept Claudine's advice, so be it; but he should at least have the intelligence to know his staff would object to being criticised by anyone other than the person who employed them. Or wouldn't the staff mind? Leggat in fact had sounded faintly amused by Claudine's behaviour and Monsieur Marcel seemed unperturbed by the thought of anyone finding something to criticise in his superbly produced meals.

Then why should she herself be so angry? The answer was obvious. Though she was here as a housekeeper, she knew it was a temporary position, and regarded herself as Mark Allen's equal and possibly Claudine Goderick's superior! But criticism, either from an equal or a superior, had never fussed her before, and she could not understand why she should feel such a strong sense of injustice even before the woman had made any criticism. Like all the questions that had been bedevilling her in the past few weeks, this one also produced an answer she did not want to bring to the surface of her mind, and she forced herself to join in the conversation around her, hoping that if she concentrated on other people, she would stop thinking about herself and her own problems. Yet why should there be any problem in temporarily working for a financial wizard? Drat the man: he was back in her thoughts again. Because he paid her salary each month there was no reason for her to think about him incessantly.

With another effort she brought her attention back to

116

Monsieur Marcel who was regaling them with an amusing if acidulated account of his two years' service with a Hollywood film star. He was in the middle of a particularly juicy episode when the bell from the drawing-room summoned Leggat away, and he returned after a moment to tell Anthea she was required to go inside.

'Nothing wrong, I hope?' she asked anxiously.

'No, miss. But I believe a friend of yours has called to see you.'

'Here?' She was startled.

'Yes, miss. Mr. Allen and some of the guests were strolling along the drive when he drove up. A gentleman in a red sports car.'

'Roger!' Anthea exclaimed. 'Oh no!' What on earth had prompted him to call on her without any warning and at this time of the night? Still, ten o'clock was not considered late among her friends, though her employer might well consider otherwise where his staff were concerned.

'Did you say my visitor was in the drawing-room?' she asked and, at Leggat's nod, hurried out.

At least Roger would not receive the same shock at her appearance as her parents had done. She grinned at the memory and glanced down at her *eau de nil* silk dress. Though she had not anticipated seeing anyone other than the staff this evening, the knowledge that a few yards away from her was a group of elegant women had spurred her into making an effort with her own appearance, almost as if she were cocking a snook at Claudine Goderick. Turning the gilded handle, she entered the drawing-room.

Havana smoke mingled with the scent of flowers and the subtle perfume of the women, whose bright dresses made splashes of colour on the maroon damask settees and armchairs and sent her thoughts winging to a production she had once seen of *Private Lives*. There was the same brittle quality in the air; the same aura of pretence and posture.

Only Roger seemed totally at ease, casual in slacks and sweater, a drink in his hand as he leaned against the wall and talked to Mark Allen and another, older man. With an assurance she did not feel she walked over to them.

'Hello there,' Roger greeted her. 'Surprised to see me?'

'Naturally. You should have warned me you were coming.'

'I didn't know it myself. I had dinner with Professor Connors, but his good lady pushed us all out at nine-thirty. You know how she fusses about the old man since his heart attack. It was too early to go to bed, so I decided to go for a spin in the car and ended up here.'

'You've a little further to go yet,' she smiled. 'Another fifty yards to my sitting-room.'

'Why the rush?' Mark Allen asked pleasantly. 'Mr. Pemberton was in the middle of telling me how he deals with student strikes.'

'He never has any,' Anthea said promptly. 'And if he did, he'd be out in front waving the flag *with* them!'

The man beside Mark Allen laughed. 'I've just heard *you* are a student too, Miss Wilmot. I must say it's very enterprising of you to take a job like this.'

'Miss Wilmot is a do-gooder,' her employer intervened. 'She's standing in for one of her friends.'

Aware of lenses glinting in her direction, and aware that Roger did not know she was acting as housekeeper and not as research assistant, Anthea put her hand on his arm. But once again she was barred from moving.

'At least have another drink before you go,' Mark Allen said to Roger.

'No more, thanks,' he replied. 'Anthea's right. I had no business barging in like this. I intended presenting myself at the tradesmen's door except that I wasn't quite sure where it was.'

'At the back of the house,' Anthea said promptly.

'Don't be annoyed with your friend.' There was no doubting the irony in Mark Allen's voice. 'He drove up as we were taking a stroll outside and we insisted he come in here for a drink. You mustn't set up old-fashioned social barriers.'

'Not social barriers, sir,' she said politely. 'The natural barrier of age.'

'Wow!' Roger grinned at his host. 'When Anthea's in one of her argumentative moods, it's best to go along with her.' He set down his empty glass on a nearby table. 'Thanks for the champagne, Mr. Allen. I hope you'll let me return the hospitality whenever you're in Reading.'

'I'd be delighted.' Mark Allen was all smiles and charm. 'The student body is one I'm not acquainted with.'

'It would be great if you would let me arrange for you to give a lecture. There's a shortage of interesting speakers.'

'I don't think anything I can say would be of interest to your students.'

'On the contrary. You're a financial whizz-kid and they'd be agog to hear you!'

'And heckle me too, no doubt,' Mark Allen smiled. 'I'm not sure I fancy qualifying for the name of Daniel!'

'I've a feeling you could take care of hecklers,' Roger replied.

'Come *on*, Roger,' Anthea intervened, anxious to terminate this conversation. Her tone and the insistent pressure of her hand on his arm drew him to the door, but only when they were alone in her sitting-room did she explode with anger.

'You had no right to come here without telephoning me first! And don't give me all that chat about just going for an aimless drive. You had every intention of coming here.'

'Is that a crime? I mean you only work here. You aren't a slave. Why can't I come and see you if I want?'

'No reason at all,' she retorted. 'But you should at least

119

make sure *I* want you to come.'

He looked so discomfited that her anger abated. After all, he had not committed a crime, and she certainly wouldn't have been so angry had he come if she were on her own. It was only because Mark Allen was here that she was disturbed. Yet he had not seemed annoyed by it; more amused than anything. She glanced at Roger, suddenly finding him young by comparison. Yet why should she compare her friends with the man for whom she was working?

'Do you fancy something to eat?' she asked.

'Pickings from the tables of the rich?' Roger grinned.

'There's a little caviar,' she grinned back. 'I can give you a couple of teaspoons of that, without it being missed.'

'What largesse!' Happily he followed her into the kitchen, empty now, for Monsieur Marcel and Leggat had retired for the night, and Anthea busied herself making coffee and setting out a plate of left-over canapés which Roger began to demolish as quickly as she set them down.

'I can see the advantages of working here,' he mumbled, his mouth full. 'This is heaps better than college grub.'

'For heaven's sake stop talking like an undergrad. You're too old for that.'

'*You*'re still an undergraduate. I just want you to remember it.'

'Meaning?'

'Meaning that our rich and fat friends in the other room are *not*.'

'They are rich,' she said evenly, 'but they're not fat. And if you object to their money, don't come along and eat their food.'

'I never thought I'd live to see *you* rooting for the bloated capitalists!'

'Very funny.' She was heavily sarcastic.

'It isn't hilarious,' he admitted, 'but it doesn't merit *such* anger.' He picked up an inch-long roll of smoked salmon and put it into his mouth. 'Haven't fallen for our whizz-kid, have you?'

'Are you mad?'

'I don't see why you say that. It's a logical assumption. He's a good-looking chap and endowed with all the assets—physical as well as financial. He's a bit too old for you, of course, but——'

'Thirty-four isn't old,' she retorted, and seeing the glint in his eyes, said hastily: '*You* aren't as young as you like to pretend. Twenty-eight last birthday, if I remember.'

'The girl remembers my age!' Roger smote his forehead. 'Perhaps she loves me after all.'

'I love you enough to tell you not to be an idiot.' Anthea sat down at the table and poured two cups of coffee.

'Am I being an idiot?' Roger asked unexpectedly. 'You've never been bothered by age or money differences before, yet you looked as if you wanted to murder me when you came into the drawing-room and saw me talking to your boss.'

She sucked in her lower lip. Roger's comment was justified and she tried to think of a reason why it should be. 'Perhaps it's because I'm only here on sufferance,' she murmured, and remembering he did not know why she had taken the job in the first place, or what she really did here—she was not sure if he had fully absorbed the sarcastic comments Mark Allen had made on the matter—she quickly told him the truth.

Roger did not hide his astonishment. 'You mean you pretended to be old and ugly?'

'Middle-aged and plain,' she corrected. 'And I would have got away with it, too, if it hadn't been for Maude.'

'Ah yes, the wicked stepmother. It's because of her that you're really here, isn't it?'

'No,' Anthea said quickly. 'I came because of Betsy Evans, though I wouldn't have stayed at home, of course.

121

But Maude isn't wicked. She's just a bit overpowering and has the finesse of a steamroller.'

Roger nodded and went on looking at her thoughtfully. 'What will you do when you leave here? October is still a long way off.'

'I'll get another job. I definitely don't want to go back home.'

'Can't whizz-kid find you something else to do? In an organisation like his, I'm sure he could manage it.'

'I don't want to go on working for him. Once I leave here I never want to see him again.'

'Why? He strikes me as a nice chap; intelligent too.'

'He's overpowering and officious,' Anthea explained. 'And he's a fool when it comes to women.'

Roger's raised brows told her she had said too much, and colour flooded her cheeks.

'Of course I'm aware of him,' she said jerkily. 'You can't work for someone for months and not be aware.'

'You *have* fallen for him,' Roger said disgustedly. 'I was right the first time.'

Anthea set her cup carefully on its saucer. Her desire to scream that Roger was wrong was a silent sound of anguish; an anguish not caused by the preposterousness of the remark but by the fact that it was staggeringly, horrifyingly true.

She was in love with Mark Allen.

She jumped up and walked over to the gas stove, where she made a pretence of seeing that all the jets were off; doing anything that would keep her face away from Roger's prying eyes. It was incredible that she had needed his jesting taunt to make her realise something her intelligence should have told her weeks ago. From the first moment she had met Mark she had been inordinately aware of him, though she had foolishly assumed it to be fear that he would see through her disguise. Instead, it had been fear of his magnetic personality which she had instinctively felt as a threat to her peace of mind. Now this peace had gone for ever; lost with the tranquil days of her youth when love was something to dream about and hope for. Now the hope was realised and the dreams had become a reality, showing her that love was no soft sweet warmth but a burning, searing pain that tormented your days and racked your nights; that stopped you from being mistress of your body and master of your desires.

'I can't love him,' she thought. 'It's impossible!' They were diametrically opposed in outlook. They had nothing in common. Yet even as she told herself this, she knew it was untrue. She and Mark had a great deal in common. She had spent enough time with him to admit this. Why hadn't she guessed that the pleasure she felt when he talked to her of the day's happenings had stemmed not only from gratification that he considered her intelligent enough to understand his problems, but also satisfaction that he wanted to share them with her? Yet his behaviour after her parents' visit had shown her how neurotically he feared being loved for his position rather than for himself, and she wondered if he had found pleasure in her company because he had believed her to be a middle-aged spinster who had wanted nothing from him, neither in the way of money or love.

'You're very quiet,' said Roger, coming to stand behind her. 'Forget what I said, Anthea. I was only teasing.'

'I've already forgotten it.'

She turned to look at him and, seeing his relief at her answer, wished with all her heart that what she had said was true. But it would take more than her desire to forget Mark Allen to really forget him. Even when she left here, it would be a long time before this house and its owner ceased to be important to her.

CHAPTER TEN

ON Sunday the weather broke. Blue skies gave way to grey and a steady drizzle blanketed the countryside. Yet it remained extremely warm, and the dampness and humidity seemed to engender a general malaise in the house-party.

For most of the morning and part of the afternoon, Mark Allen was closeted in the library with Jasper Goderick and several of the men, while the women contented themselves by playing interminable games of Canasta. On or two ventured to the sauna and a couple played a lethargic game of table tennis in the games room which had been fitted out in one of the barns.

Only Claudine seemed unconcerned by everyone else's restlessness, and as Anthea went round the bedrooms to ensure that everything was in order after the maids had finished cleaning them, she found the French-Canadian wandering along the corridor, notebook in hand. Unwilling to be forced into conversation, she retreated into the nearest bedroom and found herself in Mark Allen's. Normally when she came in to inspect it she was not conscious of it being different from any of the others, but today it took on a much greater significance. No longer was the bed an ordinary bed; but it was the one which felt the pressure of his body and the relaxation of his limbs. The dressing-table and wardrobe were not mere pieces of furniture to be examined for dust but housed his personal belongings: the silver-backed brush, the beautifully cut clothes.

Stifled by the pressure of her thoughts, she ran from the room as though bedevilled, and too late saw that Claudine was still in the corridor, scribbling in her book.

'Miss Wilmot?' the woman said in faint surprise.

'I've been inspecting the bedrooms,' Anthea said hurriedly.

'How seriously you take your duties!'

'You sound surprised.'

'I am. After all, you're not a genuine housekeeper and——'

'I'm employed as one here, and I do the work to the best of my ability. Surely that makes it genuine?'

'You know what I mean.' Claudine gave a faint smile and ran her fingers through her dark hair. The curls were soft and springy, like those on the head of a child. It was an unusual hairstyle for a sophisticated woman, yet it went well with her small features and gave her the air of a sensual Peter Pan.

'Mr. Allen told me who you really are,' Claudine went on. 'I must say I think you're very self-sacrificing to take on a job like this.'

'What's wrong with a job like this?'

'My dear, if you enjoy keeping house. . . .'

'Millions of women do.'

'Not intelligent ones.'

Anthea flushed. 'Not many people can afford to have staff these days.'

'I agree. But even so, it's possible to arrange your life without being concerned with domestic chores.'

Anthea forced herself to keep her temper, convinced she was being deliberately baited. 'Have you never kept house, Mrs. Goderick?'

'Not in the sense you mean. I didn't marry Jasper for *that*.'

As she looked at the gold circlet around Claudine's milky white throat, the reasons why she *had* married him were obvious. They were the same reasons Mark Allen feared a woman might want to marry *him*. Momentarily Anthea wondered how she would feel about him if he were

125

a university lecturer on a fixed income or ran a small business of his own. It was not easy to imagine a man of such dynamism remaining small-time for long. No matter what he did he would rise to the top of his profession. Yet what if he had chosen one which was not lucrative? Would she still want to spend her life with him? She did not need to search for the answer. What he had to offer materially was unimportant; it was what he could offer of himself that mattered. It was incredible that he did not realise his own intrinsic worth. Surely he knew the magnetism he exuded? Was aware that it would bring him almost any woman he desired? She glanced at Claudine and knew instantly that despite Mark's personality and sexual attraction, without his wealth this girl would have no interest in him whatsoever. And there were many women like Claudine. Indeed it seemed that Mark Allen's world was full of them.

'You seem very pensive, Miss Wilmot,' Claudine commented. 'I hope our being here hasn't made too much work for you.'

'We have ample staff to cope with everything,' Anthea replied composedly. 'I get far more tired when I have nothing to do.'

'You are obviously one of the world's workers. Personally, I hope Mark doesn't do any more entertaining until the house has been redecorated. Actually he won't be *able* to after next month. Jackson Pollard will be bringing in a whole team of work-people.'

'For how long?'

'A couple of months. Everything will have to be stripped and repainted; some walls are going to be knocked down and a swimming pool put in front of the terrace.'

'It might have been cheaper for Mr. Allen to buy another house,' Anthea could not help saying.

'I wish he would—I know a fabulous one that's just come on the market. But unfortunately he's attached to this one.

He likes the village, you know, and he buys any house that comes on the market in order to stop property developers from coming in and taking over.'

'What a wonderful thing to do,' Anthea said warmly.

'I should have known you'd think like that!' Claudine Goderick did not attempt to hide her amusement. 'You're not only one of the world's workers, Miss Wilmot, you're also an idealist. Do you really think a few philanthropic gestures can stop progress?'

'Property developers aren't usually interested in progress. They're interested in lining their pockets.' Anthea stopped, unsure of the ramifications of Jasper Goderick's business, and not wishing to make any comment that could be construed as a criticism of her employer's guests.

'You're reading history at university, aren't you?' Claudine enquired. 'You talk like a woolly-minded left-wing economist!'

'Do you know much about economics?' Anthea asked gently.

There was a delicate, tinkling laugh. 'After being married to Jasper for so long, I think I could teach it!' The limpid eyes had a gleam in them. 'You must be anxious to resume your own studies?'

'I am.'

'Are you a member of your university's drama society too?'

It took a moment for Anthea to realise the implication behind the question, and when she did, she gave Claudine full marks for subtlety.

'Mark thought it very enterprising of you,' the woman continued, 'the way you got the job here. You did it for a friend, I believe?'

'A woman I wanted to help,' Anthea explained.

'To begin with, Mark thought you did it as an excuse to get to know him. You'd be surprised at the ploys some girls

127

have used to bring themselves to his notice.'

'I wouldn't have thought he was difficult to meet.'

'It's easy to meet him. But getting to know him is a different story.' The gleam was noticeable in the hard eyes. 'You must admit you put yourself in an excellent position to further your acquaintance. It was a pity your subterfuge was found out. Until it was, I know he thought most highly of you. He said you were the most capable housekeeper he'd ever had.'

Anthea forced herself to look amused. 'That still applies.'

'Oh, sure, but knowing your whole manner was an act has made him suspicious of you. It's a pity really; he's already so suspicious of women.'

'When I see the ones he knows,' Anthea said, 'I'm not surprised.'

Pink tinged Claudine's cheekbones. 'You're very frank, Miss Wilmot.'

'You're very obvious, Mrs. Goderick. But I assure you that you have nothing to fear from me.'

'You don't need to tell me that!'

'Then why are you warning me off?'

'Did I say frank?' Claudine asked softly. 'Honey, you astonish me with your candour. Still, if it's candour you want. . . .' The dark head tilted. 'Don't think that because you work for Mark you'll be able to infiltrate into his life. You're young and pretty, but no prettier than hundreds of other girls.'

'Then you have nothing to worry about, have you?'

'I'm worrying for *you*, Miss Wilmot. I don't like to see anyone needlessly hurt—and your feelings have been obvious for weeks.'

'That's not true!' Anthea retorted. 'I didn't know myself until——' Too late she realised she had risen to Claudine's bait, for the woman's eyes blazed with malice.

128

'So you do love him! I guessed it even before you did. It was in your eyes—the way you looked at him.'

'It's a look you should recognise, Mrs. Goderick. I've seen it in your eyes too!'

'But *my* look is returned. That makes all the difference! Don't try to compete with me, Miss Wilmot. You're way out of your league!'

'Please,' Anthea said shakily. 'There's no point in our talking about it.' She ran a hand across a forehead that was unexpectedly damp. Why were she and Claudine talking in this preposterously intimate manner? Admitting truths that neither of them wanted to be known? Was it caused by the weather, by this deep oppressive humidity—or was it a more primitive urge—the eternal battle of woman against woman for the possession of an arrogant, uncaring male?

The sound of footsteps made them both turn, and Anthea trembled as she saw her employer coming towards them. He wore shorts and a white sweat shirt and his hair, wet with perspiration, gleamed black as a raven's wing and showed a surprising and endearing tendency to curl.

'I thought you were playing cards with the other women?' Ignoring Anthea, he spoke to Claudine.

'I've been checking through the notes I've made to give to Jackson Pollard,' Claudine linked her arm with his and pulled a face. 'Darling, you're wet as a fish.'

'So would you be after an hour of squash.'

'Did you win?'

'Of course. I never play if I think I can be beaten.'

'That doesn't only apply to squash.'

Claudine spoke softly, yet not so softly that Anthea did not hear. Feeling in the way, she moved past them, dismally aware that neither of them were conscious of her going. As far as they were concerned she did not exist.

Unable to face anyone, she went to her bedroom.

Opening the window, she leaned out. The distant river was hidden by mist, but there was the damp smell of earth in the air and of new leaves unfolding, the way her own life was unfolding. Strange that she should have fallen in love with someone as different from her expectations as Mark Allen. Contented with her life with her father, and looking only to the attainment of her degree, she had given little thought to love and marriage. When she had, she had considered that the man would be someone of her own age or just a few years older; and certainly an academic. Never in her wildest dreams had she envisaged falling for a dynamic go-getter whose calm manner was only a surface covering for a deep, overriding ambition. She wondered what had fostered such an urge to succeed, and was filled with curiosity to know everything about him.

A gust of wind blew the rain across her face, and shaking the droplets away from her lashes, she closed the window and stepped back inside the room. Two months of Jackson Pollard and his workmen! Still, Betsy Evans would be here by then and coping with the mess instead of herself. But the pleasure of the thought was marred by the anguish of knowing she would then have to leave here; would not see Mark again.

'I mustn't think of him as Mark,' she muttered. 'He's Mr. Allen. *Mr.* Allen.'

Sighing, she went down, where Monsieur Marcel was repacking all the utensils he brought with him each time he came.

'Don't you think it would be simpler to leave a complete set down here?' she suggested.

'I was going to do that, mademoiselle, then Mr. Allen told me not to bother.' The chef stopped sorting his knives and looked at her. 'A month ago he said he intended to spend more time here and asked me if I wanted the kitchen replanned. Then a week later, when I went to him with my ideas—*poof*—he had changed his mind! He is difficult to understand, that one. He begins to come here every night and then—*zut*—he only comes at weekends! I think *peut-être* he finds someone he likes in London.'

Or maybe there is someone he *dis*likes down here, Anthea thought miserably, and wondered if she was the reason why he no longer came down so frequently. The idea was depressing yet in an odd way uplifting, for she could not see why he should allow himself to be so disturbed by her behaviour if he merely regarded her as a stand-in housekeeper. Could he have grown to like her despite the fact that she had looked like a frump? More important still, could he have become fond of a girl whose very plainness presented no challenge to him, and whose acceptance of the role of housekeeper had shown a lack of greed which had commended itself to him? If the answers to all these questions were in the affirmative, then it gave her a logical reason for his extreme anger at discovering she was young and pretty and had known of his position and wealth when she had agreed to help Betsy. If only Maude and her father had not come visiting her that day! If her friendship with Mark could have progressed for several more weeks he might by then have grown to know her sufficiently well to believe in her integrity. If, if. What a waste of time it was to ponder on the might-have-beens. She was faced with the present and she could see no way of making him look at her kindly again.

'Mr. Allen wants to see you when the guests have gone,' Leggat said behind her. 'Some of them are leaving now.'

'I thought they were staying to supper?'

'This lot only like the country when the sun shines! Give 'em a bit of rain and they can't wait to get back to traffic and petrol fumes!'

'Neither can I,' said Monsieur Marcel. 'For me, London is the only place to live.' He folded his plump little hands

131

together and pursed his mouth, looking so much like a well-known detective in fiction that Anthea fully expected him to come up with a solution to her own misery or, at the very least, to give her a clue that would enable her to understand Mark Allen's complex personality.

'That reminds me,' she said to the Frenchman. 'I have a cookery book for you—an old English one written in 1840.'

'That is rare, *non*?'

Anthea nodded, and explained her father had found it in a second-hand bookshop and had given it to her for her nineteenth birthday. 'I've only done a couple of recipes from it,' she confessed, 'but some of them sound very intriguing. I'm sure you'll be able to adapt a few of them.' She went to the sitting-room and came back with a slim leather-bound volume with yellowed parchment pages.

'It is most *charmant* of you to lend it to me,' he said. 'I will treasure it with my knives.'

Since Monsieur Marcel treasured his knives as though they were the Crown Jewels, Anthea appreciated the promise and told him so. She was still smiling at the memory of his delight when she remembered Mark Allen's order to go and see him, and as she went to the library her smile was replaced by apprehension. Had Claudine complained to him of her rudeness? To have done so would have meant explaining not only what she had said, but why, and somehow she could not see the French-Canadian doing this. Briskly she knocked on the door and went in. She remained beside it, her figure—in a cream linen dress—outlined against the dark panelling, her slim legs bare.

'You wanted to see me, sir?'

'Yes. Come in and sit down.'

She moved to a chair as far away from him as possible. It was the first time she had been alone with him since knowing she loved him, and her heart pounded so loudly that it almost obliterated any other sound. I can't be in love with

132

him, she thought desperately. I don't know him or understand him. It's physical attraction—sex—nothing more than that. She peered at him from beneath her lashes. He was standing by the desk, one thigh leaning on the edge. Casually dressed in black slacks and shirt, he none the less looked as tense as a tightly coiled spring. His fingers were drumming a soft yet unceasing tattoo on the leather-topped surface, and she had the inexplicable feeling that he was going to dismiss her. That was why he looked so ill at ease.

'Mrs. Roberts—the housekeeper who looks after my London home—has been rushed to hospital with a gallstone attack,' he said abruptly. 'They're operating on her in the morning. I had a phone call from my butler half an hour ago.'

Anthea looked sympathetic but remained silent, not sure what to say.

'It couldn't have come at a worse time,' he went on. 'I've arranged dinner parties for every night of the week.'

'Can't you take your guests to a hotel?'

'Of course I can! That's not the question. The important thing is that I don't *want* to take them out to dine.' His fingers drummed faster. 'I would like you to come to London with me and take over the house until Mrs. Roberts is back in harness.'

Anthea swallowed hard. This was the last thing she had expected to hear. '*Me?*'

'Can you suggest anyone better?' His tone was dry. 'Whatever your reasons for taking the job, Miss Wilmot, you *are* my housekeeper.'

'Only at Bartham Manor.'

'If Miss Evans were here, I would expect her to look after me *wherever* I live.'

He said nothing further and Anthea knew he was waiting for her comment. There was no reply she could give other than to agree with him, and if she wanted to see Betsy Evans safely installed here, then agree with him she must. Yet the thought of living in his London home and seeing him every day filled her with dread. It was going to be difficult enough to forget him as it was; how much more difficult it would be if she became used to daily encounters.

'Would you like me to see if I can engage a temporary for you?' she asked.

'Why the reluctance to leave here?' he grated. 'London is only an hour away from Reading. I'm sure your boy-friend won't consider it a deterrent.'

She lowered her eyes, glad that he assumed her reluctance stemmed from being away from Roger. As if she cared if he lived in Tibet!

'Well,' Mark Allen pursued, 'are you worried that absence will make the heart grow wander instead of fonder?'

'It's only an hour away,' she shrugged. 'He won't wander far. Do you want me to leave for London with you in the morning, sir?'

'Yes, please. And don't call me sir!' he flared suddenly.

She stood up, her knees trembling. 'I'll be ready to leave at seven o'clock. That's your usual time, I believe.'

'Eight o'clock will be time enough.' As she turned to the door, he stopped her with a gesture of his hand. 'What were you and Mrs. Goderick talking about upstairs in the corridor?'

Not sure if the question was an innocent one, or if knowledge lay behind it, Anthea forced her tone to one of casualness. 'We were discussing Mr. Pollard. I understand he'll be taking over the Manor for a couple of months.'

'Yes. That's the best way. Do you approve of his schemes?'

'It isn't my business to approve them or not.'

'I know that!' The thin mouth widened in a mocking smile. 'But I would still like an answer.'

134

'Mr. Pollard is a good decorator,' she said evenly, 'but when the house is finished it might be more of a setting for Mrs. Goderick's personality than yours.'

The smile was wider this time. 'You're very frank.'

'That's what Mrs. Goderick said.'

'Then you *were* quarrelling?' His glasses glinted as he moved his head sharply. 'That is the sort of remark Claudine would make if someone was getting the better of her!'

'Then I should think she makes it rarely!'

He chuckled, then stopped abruptly as though annoyed with himself. 'I'll see you in the morning, Miss Wilmot.'

'Yes, Mr. Allen. Will that be all?' she asked in a toneless voice.

'Except for your salary,' he said coolly. 'While you're in London, you'll receive an increase.'

'That won't be necessary.'

'*I* am the judge of what's necessary, Miss Wilmot. As long as you're in London, you will receive the same salary as Mrs. Roberts.'

Goaded, she asked: 'What are my off-duty times, *sir*?'

'I don't know. Whenever I'm not there, I suppose.' He moved away from the desk. It brought him closer to her and she took a step backwards. 'But you're quite welcome to invite your boy-friend to visit you. I don't stop my staff from entertaining their men friends, providing it's done with discretion.'

Her cheeks flamed, but she made her voice deliberately deferential. 'I appreciate your kindness, sir. Roger isn't the type to wait outside the servants' entrance.'

Again glasses glinted. 'Is he special?'

'For the moment,' she said lightly.

'Until a new one comes along, I suppose? People of your generation don't go in for long relationships.'

'But they mean something while they last,' she retorted. 'And at least my boy-friends aren't married!'

135

His nostrils flared. 'What's that supposed to mean?'

'Nothing,' she said hastily. 'I was just making a casual remark.'

'You're backtracking fast, Miss Wilmot. Your remarks are never casual. I would like you to explain yourself.'

'I shouldn't have said it,' she replied hastily.

'But you *have*. And I insist on an explanation.' He came closer still, blocking her escape to the door. Dressed in black, with his tanned skin and dark hair, he could almost have passed for the devil, and though she knew the thought to be fanciful, she could not restrain a shiver.

'Your pr-private life is your own,' she stammered, 'but it doesn't give you the right to be critical of mine. Just be-cause—because Roger is fond of me that doesn't mean you should make snide remarks about the way I behave. How would you like it if I blamed *you* because Mrs. Goderick flings herself at your head?'

'*Don't* you blame me?' he asked. 'I have the impression you do. That you disapprove of my relationship with her.'

'I know nothing about your relationship with her!'

'That hasn't stopped you from making wild conjectures about it! Your imagination has been working overtime. I can see it in the way you glare at me. Are Claudine and I lovers, do you think? Are we having an affair beneath the eyes of her unsuspecting husband?'

'I couldn't care less if you are!' Anthea stormed. 'As long as you don't expect your housekeeper to be party to it!'

'I doubt if I'll ever need to enlist *your* aid with my love affairs, Miss Wilmot.'

'Thank heaven for that. I don't mind looking after your board, but I'm darned if I'll look after your bed!'

'Wouldn't you?' he said savagely, and reaching out, caught her roughly by her shoulders. 'Wouldn't you like to look after my bed? Sometimes I have the feeling that you

136

would!'

'How dare you?' she cried, and tried to pull away from him. 'You're crazy!'

'Am I?' His face was so close that it blocked out the rest of the room. Then his mouth came down on hers, hard and demanding, a physical reiteration of his taunting remarks.

There was no tenderness in his kiss, only a desire for satisfaction. He wanted her and he was going to have her. She tried to struggle, but he was so close she could not move, and he pinned her back against the wall, his chest crushing her breasts, his thighs hard on her hips. Because it was impossible to push him away, she tried to turn her head. But he pulled her even closer and kissed her again; the kiss deepened, arousing her to a passion she did not want to feel but which she could not prevent. A wave of desire ran through her and she felt him respond to it. His body trembled and his hands moved across her back and down to her waist; then across the rounded curve of her stomach and up to the fuller curves of her breasts. Anthea shivered at the touch of his fingers, and the movement made him lift his head away from hers. He was staring into her eyes, but as always his glasses prevented her from reading what his own eyes might say. But the beads of perspiration on his upper lip gave evidence of his emotion, though when he drew back further still and spoke to her, his voice was more sarcastic than she had ever heard it.

'I knew there was passion behind all that primness. Even in your erstwhile disguise I suspected it.'

She tried to think of a wounding retort, but no words came to mind. She was bruised by his kisses and his touch and all she wanted was to run away and hide.

'Be ready at eight in the morning,' he continued. 'I'll see you then.'

'Yes, Mr. Allen.' Her voice was soft as syrup and she marvelled that she could make it so. 'Goodnight, sir,' she continued as she walked to the door. 'I hope you sleep well.'

'The sleep of the just, Miss Wilmot. Insomnia is something that's never bothered me!'

'Nor has conscience,' she murmured, and closed the door behind her.

In the hall, she stopped and leaned against the wall, her legs too shaky to sustain further movement. What irony of fate was taking her to live in his London home? How could she bear to be in such close and constant proximity to him?

'I must learn to bear it,' she vowed, as she crossed to the stairs and slowly climbed them. 'He must never guess how I feel. Never!'

CHAPTER ELEVEN

THROUGHOUT their journey to London, Anthea sat quietly beside Mark in the back of the Rolls. He was totally engrossed in a pile of documents, and she was amazed at how easily he could forget her presence, while she sat beside him trembling at his nearness and longing to throw herself into his arms. She—Anthea Wilmot—a young and carefree girl, was suddenly finding herself carefree no longer. It was humiliating to acknowledge; the more so since she knew how amused the recipient of her devotion would be if he ever discovered it. The very thought was enough to make her shudder.

Only as they drove through the London suburbs did the man beside her rouse himself from his work to give her a brief résumé of what her duties would be. They did not appear to differ from those in the country, though with the constant entertaining which she knew he was planning, it did not look as if she would get much free time. Still, she did not wish to go out, nor did she have the head for studying. The moment she was alone with a book she started to think of Mark, and the less time she had for that, the better for her peace of mind.

Seeing her safely into the hall, with her suitcases given to a Japanese houseboy, Mark Allen drove off again, and Anthea felt so lost and lonely that she went to the kitchen to say hello to Monsieur Marcel. In his own domain he was definitely lord and master, but he greeted her with affection, a fact which seemed to please the other staff working in the kitchen, who had no doubt been wondering how the temperamental chef would receive the new housekeeper.

'It is *merveilleux* to have you *chez moi*!' he exclaimed. 'Already I have done one of the recipes from the book you gave me—a lemon syllable and truly *parfait*.'

'Syllabub,' Anthea corrected with a smile, and feeling slightly happier, followed the Japanese boy to her room.

It did not have the magnificent view of the one at Bartham Manor, but it was large and modern, with a small but beautifully equipped bathroom and a radio and television. Quickly she unpacked and then set out to inspect the house.

It was larger than she had expected, but the four floors were serviced by two lifts, one in the servants' quarters and one in the main part of the house. The kitchen was on the ground floor, but a dumb waiter fitted with an electric warming oven transported the food up to the dining-room, which was a delight to the eye with its delicately painted Chinese wallpaper and thick Chinese carpet.

Despite being rushed to the hospital, Mrs. Rogers had left a list of instructions regarding the entertainment for the week ahead, and Anthea studied the notes carefully, wondering whether Mark Allen engaged people because they fitted in with his requirements or whether they made themselves fit in order to remain with him. Either way he seemed to have everything the way he wanted it to be, both in London and the country.

By lunchtime Anthea felt she knew every detail of the running of the house. She also felt more of a housekeeper here than she did at Bartham Manor, and guessed it to be partly due to her new surroundings and partly to her finding it easier to wear a mantle of authority.

In the afternoon—with a few hours to spare—she took a taxi to the King's Road, and then walked along the crowded pavements. It was a pleasure to be among young men and women of her own age, and it was with a sense of reluctance that she finally made her way back to Eaton Square. As she did so, a dress in a boutique window caught her eye. It was leaf-green and reminded her of a tree in springtime. For a long moment she stared at it, then succumbing to temptation, went in to try it on.

Half an hour later she walked up the steps to the front door of the house, a dress box in her hands, a smile of pleasure on her face. She fumbled in her bag for the key and was still searching for it when, out of the corner of her eye, she saw the silver-grey Rolls turn the corner and draw to a stop behind her. Mark Allen's tall, lean figure emerged, bounded up to her side and opened the door.

'You're home earlier than I expected, sir,' she said breathlessly.

'My guests are arriving at six o'clock.'

'But dinner isn't until eight-thirty.'

'I realise that, Miss Wilmot. But we'll be having a business discussion beforehand.'

'Don't you ever entertain for pleasure?' she asked before she could stop herself.

'Business is my pleasure,' he said coldly, and was turning away when he noticed the box in her hands. 'Dressing up for the boy-friend?'

'Don't *your* girl-friends dress up for *you*?'

'They prefer to undress!'

He sauntered away before she had recovered her tongue

and, still gasping at his reply, Anthea went to her room.

Promptly at six the first guests arrived. Anthea did not go out to see them, but their voices told her they were male and American. Dickson, a far more austere butler than Leggat, served drinks in the drawing-room and was then dismissed and told not to return until he was rung for, a sign that the conversation was confidential. An hour later several more guests arrived, social ones this time, and the party gathered momentum, so that Anthea, busy in the butler's pantry inspecting dishes of canapés as they were taken past her, could hear the noise of talk and laughter.

It was after midnight before she got to bed, but she was too excited and tired to sleep and she lay listening to the cars as they departed. Though the house was large, it was smaller than Bartham Manor, and from her bedroom she could hear the lift that took Mark to his own suite of rooms on the floor below her. She had glanced into them briefly on her arrival and had noted the beautiful mahogany furniture, the masculine décor of dark orange and brown and the large pile of books and papers on his bedside table; even when relaxing he was still concerned with his work. She had also seen the picture of a calm-faced woman whom she had known instantly was his mother. They had the same straight nose and firm chin, but the woman's mouth was gentle, the way Mark's was on the rare occasions when he dropped his guard. It was a mouth whose touch she would never feel again, and a burning wave of longing for him trembled through her, shaming her with its force. With a moan she buried her head in her pillow.

She was dressed and downstairs before seven o'clock next morning, and though the air was warm with the hint of a lovely day to come, it did not have the freshness to which she was accustomed. She would never enjoy living in London, where the constant hum of traffic and the smell of fumes always seemed to be hovering in the air.

141

Alone in the kitchen, she took the opportunity of examining everything carefully, and marvelled at the number of gadgets at Monsieur Marcel's command: an electric knife grinder and percolator, a microwave rotisserie, eye-level ovens, a flat ceramic hob which grew hot at the press of a button and a huge deep freeze and refrigerator which stood side by side in the vast, white-tiled larder. What a great deal of money it must take to maintain this establishment: and all of it geared to the service of one man.

'Do you always make a habit of getting up so early?' Mark Allen's quiet voice made her spin round, and she saw him in the doorway, hair tousled, navy silk pyjama legs showing below a navy silk dressing gown piped in scarlet. There were no initials on the pocket, she was glad to see. There was none of his shirts either, as far as she remembered.

'What are you smiling at?' he asked.

'I was thinking that you don't sport your initials over everything.'

'I'll paint them on my Rolls if you like!' He half smiled as he ran his hands through his hair. It robbed him of some of his dignity and took ten years from his age. 'I suppose I'm too early for breakfast? I don't usually have it before eight.'

'An hour to go.' She glanced at her watch. 'But if you tell me what you like, I'll make it for you. I'm not sure what time Monsieur Marcel arrives.'

'He never prepares breakfast. That's done by Mrs. Dickson.'

Anthea flushed, annoyed with herself for not knowing this.

'Why should you know it?' he said, as she murmured an apology. 'You were engaged to look after Bartham Manor, not this place. Mrs. Dickson and her husband live in the mews flat over the garage and she comes in about seven-thirty.'

142

'You employ a lot of people.'

'You've made that comment before,' he remarked. 'I sense that you disapprove?'

'It isn't my business to approve or not.'

'A lot of things aren't your business, Miss Wilmot, but it doesn't stop you from forming opinions about them or from jumping to erroneous conclusions.'

'I could say the same about you,' she retorted, and turned away to fill the electric kettle and search along the rows of glass jars for the coffee beans.

'I take it you're referring to my remarks about you and your boy-friend?' he enquired pleasantly. 'Am I wrong in assuming that he is?'

'Yes. He's a friend—nothing more. And I have a lot of men friends.'

'You mean you play the field?'

Exasperated that he had misunderstood her, she banged the cup down on a tray. 'That wasn't what I meant at all! I have girl friends and men friends. No more, no less.' She drew a deep breath. 'You still haven't told me what you would like for breakfast.'

'Orange juice and coffee. I'm not in the mood for food.' He stifled a yawn. 'I slept like a log, yet I still feel tired.'

'That's because you overwork.' She took some oranges from the refrigerator. 'And you have another party tonight.'

'And tomorrow and the day after,' he replied. 'Which reminds me that I shall be lunching here today with Mrs. Goderick. See that there's a cold meal for us, will you? Something that we can serve ourselves, without any-one around.' He went to the door and on the threshold hesitated. 'If anyone should ever ring you—a reporter or some-one from a journal—and ask you about myself or Jasper Goderick, please tell them that you don't talk to the press.'

'Are they likely to ring me?'

He shrugged. 'They don't care whom they speak to. You

or Dickson or anyone else that they can pump.'

'I'll tell the rest of the staff,' she said. 'But what do we say if they ask about *Mrs.* Goderick?'

'I beg your pardon?'

Anthea heard the icy tone and forced herself not to react to it. 'Jackson Pollard isn't the most reticent of men. I'm sure he won't have any hesitation in telling everyone that Mrs. Goderick is choosing the décor and furnishings for Bartham Manor.'

Mark Allen took off his glasses and pressed his hand to his eyes as though they were suddenly painful. 'I never thought of that,' he muttered. 'If I ring up Pollard and tell him to keep quiet, it might make him gossip more.' He put his glasses on again and gave a faint smile. 'If anyone does ask about Mrs. Goderick, you'd better say that *all* the women I know are having a hand in the décor—including you! That should put them off the scent.'

She longed to ask him 'off the scent of what?' but knew better than to do so, and instead vented her spleen on the helpless coffee grinder.

As she was preparing to take the tray into the breakfast-room, Dickson and his wife came into the kitchen, and the butler took the tray from her and departed with it, leaving Anthea to have her own breakfast. Mrs. Dickson was far less reserved than her husband, and over cereal and eggs chatted about the way the house was run and all the visitors who came to it.

As Anthea had expected, Claudine was frequently here, though she rarely came without her husband. This reminded Anthea to order a cold lunch, and as soon as Monsieur Marcel put in an appearance she did so, also telling Dickson it was to be set out on a buffet for Mr. Allen and his guest to help themselves.

For the rest of the morning she busied herself checking the silver and linen that had been used the night before and deciding what cloth and cutlery to use tonight. Then she inspected the flower arrangements; refurbishing them with new blooms and filling some extra vases with the sheaf of carnations which had been delivered to the house that day. She placed a silver bowl of roses on the small table that stood in the bay of the drawing-room, then stepped out on to the terrace that led from it. It overlooked the paved courtyard and, like the courtyard, was full of tubs of hydrangeas and masses of flowering geraniums in pink and red.

A light step on the York stone brought her round to see Claudine Goderick staring at her in a less than friendly fashion.

'What are *you* doing here?' the woman asked.

'Admiring the flowers.'

'I can see that. I mean what are you doing in London?'

'Looking after Mr. Allen while Mrs. Roberts is ill.'

'There was no earthly reason for Mark to bring you here. Mrs. Dickson is perfectly capable of managing on her own.'

Anthea decided to take the attack into the enemy's camp. 'Why does my being here worry you?'

For an instant Claudine seemed taken aback, then with a delicate lift of her shoulders she perched on the edge of a wrought iron table, careful not to crease her beautiful beige suit. 'I don't appreciate your dislike of me, Miss Wilmot. And I have the feeling that you watch every move I make.'

It was a direct answer to a direct question, though Anthea was surprised by its candour. Had she been in Claudine's place she would never have said such a thing. 'I can assure you I haven't come here to spy on you. Mr. Allen doesn't think so either, or he wouldn't have asked me to come.'

'Mr. Allen doesn't notice you,' Claudine retorted. 'As far as he's concerned, you're just someone doing a job.'

The truth of this stung, and Anthea dug her hands into

145

the pockets of her dress, afraid lest their trembling gave her away. 'As a matter of fact I didn't want to come to London,' she said with as much candour as she could muster. 'It makes it difficult for me to see Roger.'

The blue eyes looked blank, but only for a moment. 'The young man who called to see you?' Claudine visibly relaxed. 'I thought he was charming. Naïve, but charming.'

'He's younger than you and Mr. Allen,' Anthea said guilelessly.

'Naïveté doesn't always have to do with age. I have a feeling your friend will be exactly the same when he's forty.'

'I like him that way.'

'You're similar in temperament.'

Anthea found the idea depressing but did not say so. Instead she gave a slight nod and left the terrace. She was crossing the hall when the front door opened and Mark Allen came in.

'Mrs. Goderick is on the terrace waiting for you,' she said.

With a curt nod he strode past her into the drawing-room. 'Claudine, my dear,' he called. 'I'm sorry to have kept you waiting.'

Anthea hurried out of earshot, wishing she could as easily hurry out of his life. Reluctant to give herself time to brood, she went into the kitchen. Monsieur Marcel was already busy with preparations for that evening's dinner, but Mrs. Dickson was making the staff lunch and served Anthea first —as befitted her role as housekeeper. Domestic staff had a strict code of behaviour towards each other, and the lower echelons—consisting of parlourmaid, upstairs maid, junior butler and kitchen girl—would never dream of sitting down at table with the chef, housekeeper or butler.

Immediately lunch was over Anthea went to the dining-room to inspect the table, already laid for the party. The china tonight was the most beautiful she had seen: pearl pink edged with a thick band of pure gold. The linen was pale pink too, as were the orchids that floated on shallow silver dishes down the centre of the table. She moved to straighten a fork and paused to admire the delicate gold and ivory handle. As she did so she saw a figure move on the terrace and realised that Mark and Claudine were taking after-lunch coffee there.

'Even if Jasper finds out, it won't matter!' Claudine suddenly said loudly. 'He doesn't expect me to sit at home by myself.'

'I still don't think it's wise for you to come here alone,' the man replied.

'You're worrying for nothing.'

'It isn't for nothing, Claudine. If——'

Anthea made a deliberately loud step on the parquet floor and Mark Allen stopped speaking and came across the flagstones to the open window.

'Please see that another place is laid at the table, Miss Wilmot. Mrs. Goderick will be dining here tonight.'

'Yes, Mr. Allen.' Anthea went back to the butler's pantry, angry at how easily Claudine had got her way.

So Jasper Goderick had gone out of town, leaving his young wife to kick her heels in London? What a fool he was to think she would be content to remain by herself. Surely he knew it would take more than money to keep such a woman faithful to an elderly husband? Or did he expect loyalty simply because he had bought it? He had given no indication of being jealous of Mark. Perhaps he believed that stealing another man's wife was something not done between business partners. If he did, then he would be in for a rude awakening. Depressed by the scene she had overheard, Anthea chided herself for having believed in Mark Allen's basic integrity. One protest from Claudine and his ethics had dissolved along with his will power. It took little imagination for her to visualise them as lovers, and the clarity of the vision was so painful that her eyes brimmed with tears. Resolutely she wiped them away. No man was worth crying over; this one least of all.

CHAPTER TWELVE

DESPITE her determination to stop loving Mark, Anthea found it bitter-sweet to live in daily contact with him. Since the night he had kissed her, she had become so physically conscious of him that his presence haunted her even when he was absent, and the imagination that pictured him in intimate scenes with Claudine brought those same scenes to disturb her sleep.

Jasper Goderick was in Australia, so Dickson informed her, and his wife dined at Eaton Square almost every night. She appeared to know all Mark Allen's friends, none of whom found it unusual that she should be acting as his hostess. On a few occasions Anthea heard one or two departing visitors personally thank her for a lovely evening; a compliment which the French-Canadian seemed to accept as her due. She was always the first to arrive in the evening and the last to leave at night, when her host himself drove her home. Anthea waited, sleepless, to hear his car come back; despising herself for it, she yet lacked the strength of mind not to do so. Most times he was back within half an hour, but there were occasional nights when he did not return for several hours, and it was during these times that she suffered the tortures of jealousy, cursing the vivid imagination that enabled her to picture him in Claudine's arms.

In a desperate attempt to forget him, Anthea decided to turn to Roger. He was more than willing to come to London every night, and though she made an effort to respond to his warmth and obvious desire to please her, she couldn't think of him as anything other than a friend. No amount of imagination could fire her body with desire for him. Was it a chemical attraction that made one man desirable and not another? A simple olfactory mechanism—as some scientists believed—or did it stem from a deeper reason? But no matter the reason, this attraction could not be denied, and the emotion aroused in her by one scornful kiss had unleashed something which could never be retrieved. For good or bad, Mark Allen had changed her from a girl to a woman; had filled her with desires that he alone could appease. Bleakly she admitted that she could not continue to work for him much longer. If she did not want to break down and let him know exactly how she felt about him, she would have to leave soon. Her hope that she could return to Bartham Manor for the weekend was doomed to failure, for on Friday morning he left her a note to say they would be remaining in London owing to his business commitments. Remembering she had half promised to see Roger that evening, she telephoned him at college to let him know she would not be going to the country.

'Then I'll drive up and see you,' he said.

'Don't bother calling for me,' she told him, not sure what time Mark would be home and unwilling for the two men to meet. 'I'll meet you at the Hilton.'

'It's as easy for me to call for you.'

'No,' she said quickly, and hung up before he could argue.

At mid-afternoon Mark's secretary telephoned to say he was going to the theatre but would be coming home beforehand and would like a snack. Anxious to be out before he arrived, she determined to leave the house earlier than necessary, even though it would mean having to kick her heels alone at the hotel for half an hour before Roger arrived.

Because she was not looking forward to seeing him, and felt guilty about it, she dressed with particular care, choosing a long dress of cinnamon-coloured crêpe that echoed the warm brown of her hair. The pliable material clung to every line of her figure, and she wished she owned the right kind of brassiere to wear with it.'But the neckline was cut wide and deep, making any such undergarment unpracticable. With a shrug she flung a cashmere shawl round her shoulders and went down in the servants' lift to the ground floor. Unwilling to go on a bus, she telephoned for a taxi, and hovered in the back of the hall waiting to hear it when it arrived.

She was still waiting when she saw the shadow of two men through the glass-panelled front door, and automatically went to open it. They were both of medium height and similarly dressed in navy blue suits. They each carried a briefcase, and each had closed, polite expressions. They had come to see Mr. Allen, they informed her. He was expecting them.

Remembering Mark's references to reporters, Anthea eyed them thoughtfully and then asked them to wait. Firmly closing the door in their faces, she went in search of Dickson, who told her Mr. Allen had informed him, less than an hour ago, that he was expecting two men.

Wishing to personally apologise to them for having left them on the doorstep, she hurried back upstairs and escorted them into the library. Their air of quiet authority convinced her they were officials of one sort or another, and she was puzzling over it as she returned to the hall to wait for her taxi. Again she saw broad shoulders framed in the doorway, but this time it was Mark Allen, looking more than usually fatigued.

'There are two men waiting to see you,' she said softly as he came through the door. 'They're in the library.'

He nodded but made no attempt to move, and she saw

that apart from looking tired, he was also pale. 'Would you tell Dickson that if anyone rings for me he is to say I'm not at home.'

'Yes, sir.'

He moved towards the library, his step so slow that she felt he was reluctant to face the men who were inside.

'Is anything wrong?' she asked impulsively.

'No.' His tone was sharp and he swung round and gave her a searching look. As he did, he seemed to notice her appearance, and his eyes moved from her creamy throat to the soft shadow between the curve of her breasts. 'If you're on your way out, Miss Wilmot, don't let me delay you.'

'I'm early anyway.' She hesitated. 'I'm waiting for a taxi.'

'Cancel it and let Herbert drive you'.

'Do you normally let your chauffeur drive your house-keeper?'

'You're not a normal housekeeper.' His eyes strayed over her body. 'Where are you going?'

'To the Hilton.' She looked away from him. 'With Roger.'

'The ever-willing friend! Bring him back here after-wards if you like. I have no objection. I'm sure you're al-ways circumspect.'

'You have visitors waiting for you in the library, sir,' she said coolly, ignoring his offer.

Immediately his expression hardened, and with a sigh he opened the door and closed it quickly behind him, shutting off the sound of the voices that greeted him, but not before she heard him say, 'Good evening, Inspector.'

She was still puzzling as to what this meant when she met Roger at the Penthouse Bar, and it required a conscious effort to put her employer from her mind. Eventually the good food and wine did what Roger's presence alone could never have done, and dancing with him on the small but not

151

too crowded floor, Anthea could almost lull herself into a sense of contentment and a belief that she would be able to find a reasonably happy future, if not with this man, then with one of a similar type.

But Roger's attempts to make love to her in the confines of his car, later that night, destroyed this belief, and though she forced herself not to push him away she could not force herself to respond.

Exasperated by her lack of ardour, he was unexpectedly angry. 'What's the matter with me, Anthea? Do I repel you?'

'Of course not! There's nothing the matter with *you*, Roger. It's me, I guess. I'm just not in the mood.'

'You never are.'

'You're exaggerating,' she said lightly, and got out of the car.

'Not the back entrance tonight?' he asked, his good humour returning as he came with her up the steps and waited while she searched for her key.

'It's in the mews, and I don't like going there late at night.'

'Not even with me to protect you?'

'Particularly with you!'

'I'm glad to hear you're at least afraid of me. It gives me hope for the future. The one thing you haven't yet said is that you look on me like a brother!'

'But I do,' she retorted. 'My favourite brother!'

He chucked her under the chin and she giggled, the sound dying as the door opened and Mark Allen stood there, his face frigid.

'I would rather you didn't do your entertaining on the doorstep, Miss Wilmot.'

She flushed scarlet. 'Roger is just going,' she said, and gave him a slight push down the steps.

'Same time, same place on Monday?' he called.

'No.'

'Tuesday, then?'

Aware of Mark still beside her, Anthea nodded—she could always telephone Roger later and opt out of the arrangement—and watched with relief as he drove away with a roar of the exhaust.

'I'm sorry about that,' she apologised, stepping into the hall. 'I didn't think you would be home so early.'

'I didn't go out.'

With surprise she saw he was still wearing the suit she had seen earlier that evening, and glancing through the half open door of the library saw a thick haze of tobacco smoke. 'You haven't been with those men the whole time?' she burst out.

'Yes. And I'm exhausted.'

'Have you had dinner?'

'Sandwiches. The Dicksons had gone out for the evening —as *I* was supposed to do—and I got one of the maids to prepare something.'

'Would you like me to make you an omelette?'

'No, thanks.' He moved towards the library, but though his words were incisive his footsteps faltered. She longed to run over and hold him, but forced herself to remain where she was, though nothing could prevent her from speaking. 'Do let me make you a hot drink, Mr. Allen. Sit down and I'll bring it in to you.'

She hurried to the kitchen before he could stop her. There was some chicken broth in the refrigerator and she heated it up while she made an omelette and set it on a hot, covered plate. Then she took the tray into the library.

He looked at it and frowned. 'I told you I didn't want anything to eat.'

Ignoring him, she set the tray on a small table and drew it towards him. In normal circumstances she would have left him to eat alone, but an urge stronger than she could control made her perch on the edge of a chair and deliber-

153

ately stare at the tray. With a sigh he picked up the soup spoon and drank, then tackled the omelette. He ate three-quarters of it before setting down his knife and fork and pushing the tray away. He looked less tired, but when he took off his glasses to rub his eyes she saw that they were red-rimmed.

'Don't put them on again,' she said quickly as he went to do so. Surprised, he stopped with his hands in mid-air and she said hastily: 'I'm sure it will do your eyes good to rest them for a while. I was always told people shouldn't wear their glasses all the time.'

'I bet you just made that up.'

'How did you guess?'

'Because you're occasionally as transparent as a sheet of glass!'

'Not as breakable, I hope?'

'Perhaps I should have said toughened glass. That's what all women are made of. It's the men who shatter easily.'

'You always talk rot when you start generalising.' She drew a sharp breath. 'I'm sorry, I shouldn't have said that. I keep forgetting I work for you.'

'I forget it too.' His look was oblique. 'It will be strange when your replacement takes over. I don't suppose you'd care for the job on a permanent basis?'

Her heart thumped, but she kept her voice low: only in that way could she prevent it from sounding shaky. 'You'd be horrified if I accepted. You're just suggesting it because you're tired.'

There was a short silence before he spoke. 'You're quite right, Miss Wilmot. I don't mean it.'

The finality in his voice filled her with depression and she stood up.

'What's the hurry?' he enquired.

'I thought you wanted to go to bed. You look tired.'

'I am. But too tired to sleep. It's been a gruelling evening.'

'Is anything wrong?'

'I'm afraid so.'

Mark didn't elaborate and she knew better than to ask him what he meant. But she could not stop one comment escaping her. 'They were policemen, weren't they?'

His head lifted and his eyes stared at her myopically, dark grey and shining. 'Fate plays strange tricks,' he murmured, and she knew he was speaking to himself rather than to her. 'You work for years to create an empire and then you find it's built on shifting sand. You try to strengthen it with concrete—steel—anything you can get your hands on—but nothing you can do can stop it from collapsing, and all the work of a lifetime is destroyed. I don't know what's worse, Anthea; to destroy yourself or to destroy another person.'

'Most people would rather destroy another person,' she said steadily, and wondered if he knew he had called her by her Christian name. 'It really depends on your conscience.'

'You need to be very rich or very poor to be able to afford a conscience,' he said carefully.

'*You* are very rich.'

He sighed and leaned his head on the chair back. 'Would you like to put on some music? The tape deck is behind me. Choose anything you like.'

She went to the shelf and looked along the line of tapes before choosing the Elgar Violin Concerto. The hauntingly plaintive notes filled the room and she remained behind Mark's chair, seeing the light of the standard lamp shining on his hair and resisting the urge to run her hand through it. She came round the side of the chair and as she did, his fingers reached out and caught hers. The movement swung her off balance and she stumbled. His hand tightened and he pulled her on to his lap and sought her mouth, kissing her as though all along he had been hungry for her touch.

155

She tried to resist him, but it was hopeless and with a little sigh she gave in to him. Her arms crept around his neck and her lips moved beneath his as she responded to his urgency without holding back. Around them the music swelled and reverberated, but they were lost in a world of their own making: mouth on mouth, limb against limb, breath intermingling with breath.

It was a long time later when she shakily moved off his lap. The top of her dress had slipped down and there were the faint marks of his touch on her breasts, which still throbbed with desire for him. He stood up and lowered his head until his lips rested against one pink mark.

'You'd better go to bed,' he said huskily, 'while I can still let you go there alone.'

The presumption that she would not stop him wounded her, and she hit out at him in the only way she could.

'Don't read too much in a kiss. My generation doesn't take it as seriously as yours, remember.'

He straightened immediately. 'Don't confuse passion with permanence,' he drawled.

'Especially as permanence is the last thing you want,' she added. 'You're wise to stick to married women!'

His answer was a derisive laugh and it echoed in her ears as she slammed the door behind her and ran to the safety of her room. His kisses tonight, unlike the ones he had given her before, could not be so quickly dismissed. These were kisses to which she had openly responded, and she was honest enough to admit that it was his control rather than her own which had stopped her from final surrender. The knowledge should have horrified her, yet her only regret was that now she would never know the happiness of complete fulfilment with him. How much she loved him! How deeply she ached to comfort him and how terribly frightened she was for what the future might hold in store for him.

Trembling, she sat on the bed and remembered what he

said about building an empire on shifting sand. She did not know how he had begun his meteoric rise to success but was half aware it had come about solely from his own efforts. Were there shadows in his past which were now casting shadows on the present? From what he had said it looked as if the entire edifice he had created was going to come crashing down on him. But if this were so, why was he having merger talks with Jasper Goderick? Was it an attempt to ward off public suspicion while he tried to retrieve his lost fortunes, or was he hoping to be bought out and to save something from the débâcle?

If only she were more cognisant of the true facts of his work instead of relying on intuition and a small amount of knowledge. Poor Mark. Without power and success, what would his future be? Would he have the courage to begin again, and would Claudine remain with him? The thought of Claudine almost destroyed her pity for him—but not quite—and the tears that poured down her face were not just for her own unrequited love but for all that he himself seemed about to lose.

In the morning Anthea telephoned Chrissy and asked her to go and see Betsy Evans and find out how long it would be before she was able to start work.

'I saw her last night,' Chrissy said, 'and the doctor told her she could begin in a fortnight. There's no trouble about the job, is there, Miss Anthea?'

'No trouble at all,' Anthea said hastily. 'I was just checking to make sure how much longer I'd have to stay on.'

'Getting fed up, are you?'

'A bit. I—I miss my friends.'

'Well, it won't be long before you're back home,' Chrissy replied comfortingly. 'I take it you *will* be coming home?'

'Not permanently, Chrissy. Only till I find a place of my own.'

Anthea hung up. Two more weeks before Betsy could take over. She was not sure she had the strength of mind to remain here that long. Yet not to stay might make Mark suspicious of her feelings. He was too astute not to guess her reasons if she suddenly said she was leaving.

With an enormous effort of will power she went about her normal duties. It was a pity they were spending the weekend here instead of at the Manor, where she would have been far less likely to bump into him. The prospect of an unexpected encounter was so nerve-racking that at noon she deliberately went in search of him.

He was at his desk in the library, surrounded by the inevitable plethora of documents. He looked as if his night had been as sleepless as her own, and he rose as she came in, the first sign he had ever given that she was a woman and not his housekeeper.

'About last night——' she began in a rush.

'I owe you an apology,' he said, before she could continue. 'I intended to tell you first thing this morning, but I got caught up with work. I'm extremely sorry for what happened. I promise you it will never occur again. My only excuse is that I was tired and upset. It made me susceptible to your—to your.... You're very beautiful,' he concluded.

Remembering her unashamed response to his lovemaking, Anthea said: 'Nerves can play havoc with one's senses. *I* was upset too. I suppose it was because I'd been out with Roger and I—I must have missed him.'

'I hope I was not too inadequate a stand-in?' he questioned, reverting to his usual sarcasm.

'You weren't inadequate at all,' she said brightly. 'You were so good that I think it might be dangerous for us to repeat the performance.' She looked at the floor. 'Miss Evans hopes to start work for you in a couple of weeks. I'll stay here until then, but it would be best if we saw as little as possible of each other.'

'As you wish. But as I said before, you need have no fear that there will be a repetition of last night.'

He sat down again and picked up his pen, not raising his head as Anthea opened the door and went out.

In the evening Mark dined at home with Claudine and spent Sunday with her too, closeted in the library. He made no attempt to hide the documents on his desk from her, and Anthea wondered whether he had told the woman what might be happening. The glimpse she had of Claudine provided no answer, for she looked as beautiful and composed as always.

It was only Mark who looked haggard, and as the following week went by, this was accompanied by unusual irritability. His mood subtly affected the household, as if everyone was responding to his worries though they were not even aware that he had any. But it made tempers run high, and Monsieur Marcel sharpened his knives with extra ferocity, while Dickson became more reserved than ever.

A prey to anxieties of her own, Anthea decided not to put off her date on Tuesday with Roger. It would do her good to go out with someone who was totally unaware of the problems she was having to cope with. If she could pretend hard enough that she was having a good time, perhaps she might actually start to believe it.

But it was harder to put on an act than she had realised, and halfway through dinner Roger bluntly asked what was wrong with her.

'The university,' she lied. 'I'm not sure I'll be able to put my mind to studying. It's been more than a year since I gave it up.'

'But you were doing research for your father for most of that time. I bet you're not half as rusty as you think.'

'I wish *you* were my tutor,' she smiled. 'I'd have no worries then!'

'You've got no worries now,' he said firmly. 'You're the brainiest and brightest girl I know.'

'You wouldn't like to put that in writing, would you!'

'Do you need affirmation? Where's all your confidence gone, sweetheart?'

'Down the sink, I'm afraid. The sooner I quit housekeeping the better.'

'Amen to that,' he replied. 'I knew it would get you down sooner or later. Next time you take on the duties of running a house, make sure it's your own—or better still, mine!' He leaned across the table. 'Any chance?'

She shook her head. ''Fraid not. Just friends, Roger, nothing more.'

He accepted the rebuff with grace, but later as he drove her back to Eaton Square, he returned to the subject. 'I still hope to make you change your mind about me. I love you, Anthea, and until I know you're in love with someone else, I won't give up.'

It was a temptation to tell him that she was; it would at least stop him from wasting his time. But pride kept her silent. It was bad enough to love a man who saw her only as an irritating female with an occasional ability to arouse him, without openly admitting this to anyone else.

'How are you fixed for Wednesday evening?' Roger continued.

The thought of another evening of pretence was more than she could bear at the moment, and she murmured that she was not sure what her employer's plans were but would phone him as soon as she knew. 'But I'll be back in Reading in a fortnight,' she assured him, 'and I'll see you then.'

'Try and make it before. I don't want to wait two weeks.'

Silently acknowledging that the next time she saw him would be the last—she had definitely decided it was unfair to go on seeing him when she did not reciprocate his feelings—Anthea let herself into the house and was about to lock the door when she heard voices in the drawing-room. Claudine had not yet gone. Anthea glanced at her watch and frowned. It was lucky Jasper Goderick did not know his wife was such a frequent visitor here.

Unwilling to use the lift and make a noise, Anthea climbed the stairs to the top floor. But once she was in bed, sleep refused to come, and she tossed and turned the next hour away. At three o'clock an even greater restlessness sent her downstairs to the kitchen to make herself some hot milk.

She was in the butler's pantry when she heard a noise coming from the main hall. The hair on her scalp prickled and she tilted her head and listened. Yes, there was definitely someone in the front part of the house. She tiptoed to the green baize door and inched it open. Her heart was pounding and she wished she had something heavy to hold instead of this ridiculous glass of milk. She looked around, but there was not even a walking stick in sight; nothing but a gilt console table and a pair of spindly-legged chairs which, if used as a weapon, looked more likely to collapse into pieces than to knock anyone unconscious.

'I can't stay with him any longer! Help me, Mark. You're the only one who can.'

The words—poignant and dramatic—stopped Anthea dead, and with horror she realised that what she had taken to be a burglar was in fact Claudine. She must have gone to the cloakroom—those were obviously the soft footsteps she had heard—and now had returned to the drawing-room and left the door ajar. Yet how late it was for her to be here! Didn't she care about her reputation?

'You can't leave Jasper yet.' Mark was speaking, his voice as insistent as Claudine's. 'It's important that he doesn't suspect anything for the moment.'

'How much longer do I have to stay with him?'

'I'll let you know when it's safe to leave.'

'Are you sure he doesn't suspect?'

'Positive.' Mark was incisive. 'That's why you've got to stay with him for the time being. Everything depends on it.'

'Oh, Mark!' Claudine's voice was full of tears. 'I don't know what I'd do without you. If only——'

Anthea did not wait to hear any more. Swiftly she turned away, and as she did so, the telephone rang. The sound was so unnerving that she stopped, transfixed. Who could be ringing at such an hour? A transatlantic call for Mark, perhaps—or was it Maude to say something had happened to her father? Still rooted to the spot by fear, she heard the ringing cut off and Mark's voice, abrupt and loud. It was impossible to make out the conversation, but it ended in a matter of seconds and she heard him speaking to Claudine.

'It was your maid. Jasper's come home!'

'At this time of night? That's impossible! He was in Australia. Planes don't arrive at this hour.'

'He got in a few minutes ago. It sounds as if he left it deliberately late before coming back from the airport. The maid said he asked where you were and——'

'She didn't say I was here?' Claudine asked shrilly.

'She told him I collected you this evening and that we went out to dinner. He's on his way here now.'

Claudine's gasp was audible. 'He mustn't find me here so late! He'll be furious. You know how insanely jealous he is. He'll never believe we were just sitting here talking.'

'Particularly as we can't tell him what we were talking about.' Mark swore angrily. 'I told you to go home hours ago.'

'I know—and I'm sorry. But what can we do now? Jasper will be here any minute. Oh, God!'

There was the sound of steps across the carpet and Anthea turned swiftly and ran towards the servants' hall. But again she was stopped by a ring, only this time it was the doorbell, followed almost immediately by the knocker. It reverberated through the hall as though the man outside intended to break his way in. The drawing-room door was flung wide and Mark stood there, Claudine behind him, pale as a ghost.

'What in heaven's name are *you* doing here?' he said to Anthea.

'I came down for some milk.' She was overwhelmingly glad that the glass in her hand gave truth to her statement. 'I heard voices and thought it was a burglar. Then the bell rang and——'

The knocker crashed again and Claudine jumped. 'It's Jasper! If he finds me here he'll——'

'We can't just let him stand there,' Mark cut in. 'You'd better hide.' His glasses glinted as his head turned in Anthea's direction again. 'Hide in Anthea's room. He'll never look for you there.'

'If he sees you haven't gone to bed yet he'll know I'm here,' Claudine cried. 'He'll search the house!' Her voice rose higher with every word. 'You don't know what he's like, Mark. He's insanely jealous of me. He might even have a gun!'

'Be quiet!' cried Mark, and catching Claudine by the shoulders, pushed her towards the butler's pantry. 'I'll try and keep Jasper talking as long as I can. You get out of the house and make for home.'

'I can't go home now,' Claudine sobbed. 'He'll want to know where I've been. I'll go to Mimi Pollocks. I've sometimes spent a night there when Jasper's been away.'

'Then get there as fast as you can.'

'I'll show you the back way out,' Anthea put in, and caught Claudine by the arm.

'It won't work,' said Claudine, swinging round to Mark. 'Not if he sees you're still up.'

'I'll say he was with me,' Anthea rushed in, and looked directly at Claudine. 'Go down the servants' hall past the kitchen to the back door. It's locked and bolted, but you'll find the key hanging on the wall beside it. You can slip out through the courtyard to the mews—you should be able to find a taxi there. If your husband sees *me* with Mr. Allen, he won't suspect anything.'

Claudine nodded, and clutching her bag, ran down the corridor. Behind her the knocker crashed again and as Mark moved across to answer it, Anthea raced into the drawing-room and flung herself on the settee, noting drearily that its pillows were already dented. She heard the bolt slide back and then Jasper's voice rasping and suspicious.

'I've come for my wife. I know she's here.'

'Claudine?' Mark sounded incredulous. 'Is this your idea of a joke? I left her hours ago.'

'Don't give me that! She isn't at home and I know she's——'

'I dropped her off at Mimi's,' Mark interrupted.

'At where?' Jasper stopped, still suspicious.

'At Mimi Pollocks'. She's a friend of your wife's; surely you know her? Claudine said she often stays there when you're abroad.'

'She's *here*,' Jasper insisted. 'You can't fool me. She's been making eyes at you for months—and you haven't been unaware of *her* either!'

'If you're suggesting I'm having a love affair with your wife——'

'That's exactly what I'm suggesting!' Jasper bellowed, 'and I'm coming in to prove it.'

His steps rang out in the hall and Anthea sprawled across the settee. She clutched her dressing gown around her as the door was flung wide and the Australian rushed in. At the sight of Anthea he stopped dead. Then he shook himself like a dog coming out of water.

'You're not—you aren't—where's my wife?'

'How should I know?' Anthea made her voice faintly insolent, and deliberately pulled her dressing gown tighter as though to indicate that she wore only a flimsy nightdress underneath it. 'I've been here with Mark—Mr. Allen—since he came in.'

'*You?*'

Anthea glanced at Mark, who had come into the drawing-room, and then held out her hand to him in a half pleading gesture.

'This is awfully embarrassing, Mark. I didn't expect your friend to burst in on you in the middle of the night.'

'Neither did I,' he drawled, and shot an amused look at Jasper. 'Go home, old chap, and get a good night's sleep. Or if you'll rest easier, go and wake up Mimi. I'm sure she'll be delighted to give you a four a.m. cup of coffee!'

Jasper shook his head again. 'I'm sorry Mark, I—I don't know what got into me. But when I'm away from Claudine I always think. ... She's beautiful and young, and I——'

'There's no need to explain.' Mark was the epitome of the understanding host, and Jasper showed equal understanding as he gave Anthea a leer that could not be misinterpreted and which sent a wave of heat coursing through her body.

'I'm sorry for interrupting you, Mark. I hope you'll forgive me.'

'I'll answer that tomorrow,' Mark smiled, and leaned negligently against the door as Jasper muttered another apology and hurried from the house. Only as the sound of his car died away did he straighten and come into the centre of the room. As always it was difficult to read his expression because of his glasses, but there was no doubting the quirk of amusement that lifted the side of his mouth.

'The stage has lost a great actress in you, Anthea. And such imagination too!'

'It saved your skin,' she said coldly and, now that the danger had passed, felt like a mother who had seen her

165

child narrowly miss death. Only by hitting him could she relieve the tension. 'Perhaps you might have found it more amusing to see your name splashed in the newspapers?'

'It might happen even yet,' he replied. 'You don't think Jasper will keep quiet at finding *you* here with me at this hour of the night?'

'What do you mean? I work for you,' she retorted.

'Indeed you do; and in a very fetching dressing gown if I may say so. I'm afraid Jasper's going to regale his cronies with this little titbit.'

'But he couldn't! Not with a wife like——' She set her lips tightly together, but the man in front of her knew what she had been going to say.

'Thanks to your quick wits, my dear, Jasper now believes Claudine to be as pure as driven snow. It will give him double pleasure to turn *you* into the scarlet woman.'

Anthea shivered. In her efforts to save Mark from Goderick's fury, she had given no thought to what she was doing to herself. Now that she did, she saw it was too late to change the course of events. The thought of her father's distress was uppermost in her mind as she spoke. 'Even if Mr. Goderick does gossip about—about finding me here with you, it wouldn't get into the newspapers, would it?'

'It might. Men like me are considered fair game by newshounds.' He rubbed his hand across his chin and looked at her speculatively. 'I'm surprised you consider the publicity so disagreeable. After all, as a member of the free-thinking younger generation——'

'I don't care for myself,' she intervened. 'I'm thinking of my father!'

The sardonic expression left his face. 'I'm sorry, I'd completely forgotten your family. But I didn't ask you to rush to my defence, you know, although I greatly appreciate the fact that you did.' He crossed his arms on his chest. 'I'm sure it wasn't to save Claudine.'

Unwilling to say she had done it for him, yet equally unwilling to pretend she had done it for Claudine, Anthea remained mute.

'There's only one way to prevent any gossip,' he said in the silence. 'We can pretend you're my fiancée. I believe engagements these days are often regarded as being as good as marriage, and certainly if you were my future wife your being with me in your dressing gown at three in the morning wouldn't arouse much comment—if any at all.'

'Are you proposing to me?' she asked sharply.

'Only as a temporary measure.'

She averted her head. To have him propose to her was something she had never envisaged, and to have him do it as a pretence filled her with a bitterness tangible enough to be swallowed away. 'How long would we have to—to pretend for?' she asked.

'Does it matter?'

'Of course it matters. You don't think I want to be your fiancée, do you, any more than you want to be mine?'

'It might have its compensations.' Mark's eyes moved across her and she straightened her shoulders to stop her dressing gown from sagging.

'I would have to explain to Roger,' she said swiftly, 'and you would have to explain to Mrs. Goderick.'

'We'll both have explanations to make.' He was icily polite. 'But I take it you're agreeable in principle?'

'If *you* had any principle,' she said bitterly, 'we wouldn't be in this predicament now.'

He yawned. 'Halfway to dawn and you're as sharp as ever. You'll make a bitch of a wife for some unhappy man!'

Anthea jumped up and had reached the door when his drawling voice arrested her. 'If we announce our engagement to the press tomorrow, you can't continue as my housekeeper.'

'But I——'

'And I'll have to ask my aunt to stay here with us as a chaperone. It will save you moving out.' His eyes glinted. 'Or did you think I was going to let you rush back to Reading?'

Furious at his teasing, yet strangely elated to know she could go on living here, she merely shook her head and ran from the room, afraid that if she remained she would burst into tears and throw herself into his arms. At last she was engaged to the man she loved. Engaged until such a time as he was able to openly admit his love for another woman.

CHAPTER THIRTEEN

MARK ALLEN'S engagement was a nine days' wonder. The tabloids made reference to Anthea having worked as his housekeeper, but the more sober papers referred to her as a university student and the daughter of Professor Wilmot, the well-known historian. There were several extremely flattering photographs of her, and one where Mark had his arm across her shoulders and was regarding her with deep affection. And he had the audacity to comment on *her* acting ability!

Lady Wittle was delighted to install herself in Eaton Square. Her nephew had apparently not told her his engagement was a pretence, and Anthea was forced to listen to the woman talking to her about wedding plans and the future great-nephews and nieces she envisaged being able to spoil.

'I've waited so long for Mark to get married,' she said, 'and I'm absolutely delighted he had the sense to choose *you*.'

'We aren't married yet,' Anthea replied, and seeing Lady Wittle's startled glance, added: 'I'm superstitious. I don't like talking about the future.'

'There's no need to be superstitious with Mark's ring on your finger.' She glanced at Anthea's hand. 'Which reminds me, where *is* your engagement ring?'

'I haven't got one. Everything happened so quickly that I—I don't think Mark has had time to buy one yet.'

'If I know my nephew, he bought the ring the moment he made up his mind about you. And I'm pretty sure that was as soon as he saw you!'

Remembering the long black dress and the screwed-back hair, Anthea found this difficult to believe, and said so.

'Nonsense,' Lady Wittle replied. 'It didn't take *me* long to recognise your potential. Besides, I doubt if it was your looks that Mark fell in love with; I think it was those bright intelligent eyes and that lively mind of yours. Anyway, it takes more than an old-fashioned dress to hide sex appeal.'

'How right you are!'

Both women turned to see Mark advancing towards them.

'You're home early,' his aunt said affectionately.

'I have a business meeting here.' He glanced at Anthea and she noticed that behind his smile his expression was strained. 'It may go on most of the evening, so you'd better be prepared to amuse yourselves.' He came across to Anthea and pulled her against his side. 'How about a kiss for a weary man?'

Aware of Lady Wittle watching them, Anthea had no choice but to comply. Mark's lips were cool on hers, but as they felt the warmth of her mouth their pressure increased and she felt his arm tighten around her. Firmly but insistently she pulled away and made a pretence of smoothing her hair in front of the mirror.

'I feel I'm inhibiting you,' said Lady Wittle, and ignoring Anthea's protests, walked out.

As the door closed behind her Mark spoke. 'You're not

always a good actress, are you? You should at least pretend you want to be alone with me.'

'I don't see any reason why you can't tell your aunt the truth.'

'The less people who know the truth the better. It's imperative that Jasper doesn't find out.'

'Do you think he would come and shoot you?' Anthea asked scornfully. 'Or do you honestly believe Claudine will stay with him for ever?'

'Claudine will leave him when——' He stopped abruptly. But he had said enough to destroy Anthea's illusionary pleasure in her pretended engagement, reminding her again that she was merely being used as a cover.

'Will you marry Claudine when she's free?' she asked.

'Are you really interested in my future or just curious?'

'Neither,' she said airily. 'I couldn't care less what you do.'

He stared at her broodingly and then put his hand in his pocket and withdrew a ring case. 'For you,' he said laconically.

She lifted the lid and, expecting to see a large if banal diamond, was entranced by a magnificent emerald. She slipped it on her engagement finger. 'It's beautiful . . . beautiful! But surely it wasn't necessary to get something so expensive?'

'It belonged to my mother. I had it made smaller to fit you.'

Her reply was forestalled by the arrival of Mark's visitors, and though she did not go with him as he left the drawing-room, she glimpsed their figures through the open door and saw it was the same two men she had let into the house the week before. One of them was an inspector, she remembered, and wished she had the courage to ask Mark what was wrong. She pushed back her hair and as she did so saw the ring on her finger; his mother's ring. How strange that he should have gone to the trouble of having it made

170

smaller. Or would he have had to do so for Claudine anyway? Somehow she could not see this ring appealing to the French-Canadian, whose taste in jewellery ran to the baroque. But then men in love were often blind, and Mark might well think that because the ring had been his mother's, it would hold a sentimental value for Claudine.

As he had feared, Mark was not free to dine with her and his aunt, and they ate in the breakfast-room and then remained there to watch television. Anthea arranged for cups of soup and smoked salmon sandwiches to be served in the library. Although she was no longer the official housekeeper it seemed silly not to continue supervising the house.

'Are your parents pleased at your engagement?' Lady Wittle asked as the news headlines came to an end.

'I haven't seen them to speak to—they've rented a small villa in Portugal for a month—but they wrote and said they're delighted.'

This part of the subterfuge was the one Anthea disliked most. But Mark had insisted she maintain the pretence with them too, and she recognised his continuous attention to detail as one of the reasons for his success in business. Nothing was too small for him to acquaint himself with, yet he also had the capacity to delegate. It was an unusual combination. She bit back a sigh. But then he was an unusual man. Only by falling in love with the predictable Claudine had his intelligence failed him.

At ten o'clock Lady Wittle retired to her room, but Anthea was too restless to follow suit and, conscious of Mark still in the library with his visitors, remained downstairs. It was nearly midnight before she heard the front door close and Mark's steps move across to the elevator. There was a pause and she guessed he had seen the light in the breakfast-room. The door opened and he came in.

'I thought you'd be in bed by now.'

'I wasn't tired.' She looked at him. 'I can see *you* are.

Would you like me to get you something?'

'Nothing to drink, thanks. I'm awash with coffee and brandy.'

'Who were the men?' she asked casually.

'Just men,' he shrugged.

'What did they want? This is the second time they've been here in a week.'

'Do you keep a note of everyone who calls to see me?'

'I happened to notice those two.' His fatigue gave her courage. 'One of them is an inspector, isn't he? I heard you say so the first time he came here. What do the police want with you, Mark?'

'So many questions,' he said with a slight smile. 'You don't expect me to answer them?'

'Why not? I'm your——' she stopped, discomfited to know she had been about to say she was his fiancée, and aware from the tight look about his mouth that he realised it.

'Are you my fiancée?' he questioned. 'And would you be as willing to know and share my problems if I were destitute? Or are you like the rest of your sex, interested only in security and capturing a rich husband?'

'I wouldn't have you, rich *or* poor,' she retorted and, intent on wounding him, added: 'I would hardly call Roger a millionaire.'

'True,' he agreed, 'but he does command a fair amount of respect in university circles, and women like that too. Riches and esteem. Both if you can get it; one or the other if you can't.'

'Why are you so cynical about women?' she could not help asking.

'I thought my aunt might have told you?' One dark brow raised. 'I was engaged many years ago and was jilted for someone richer. It spurred my ambition—for which I'm suitably grateful to my ex-lady-love—and of course she followed the usual course and offered herself to me again when she felt I could afford her. Unfortunately she was married by that time, and I didn't find the proposition attractive.'

'I thought you preferred married women?'

He stretched and yawned. 'Go to bed, Miss Anthea Wilmot, your claws are showing.'

'Yes, Mr. Mark Allen, *sir*.'

His eyes gleamed. 'One day I'll——' He stopped. 'Good night, Anthea. Sleep well.'

Anthea was in the drawing-room the next morning when Jackson Pollard arrived to see her, apologising for not having made an appointment but saying he had been with another client close by and had called on an impulse. She pretended to believe him and waited for him to get to the reason for his call, which he did with the ease she had come to expect from him.

When he had read of her engagement, he informed her, it had struck him she might wish to make alterations to the schemes Mrs. Goderick had approved for Bartham Manor. By chance he happened to have the colour charts and swatches of material with him, and if she would like to look at them he would be delighted to change anything to suit her.

Anthea's first inclination was to say she would leave things as they were, but an imp of mischief prompted her to take advantage of the situation she was in. It would serve Claudine right. Carefully she scrutinised all the layouts the interior decorator had prepared. The major structural alterations could not be bettered, but there were many colour schemes she considered either too feminine or too urban for the manor house, and these she ruthlessly changed.

'I see you want it as a country home,' Jackson Pollard stated.

'It *is* a country home.'

The blond head wagged approvingly and more swatches of material were brought out from the valise. Two hours later the man departed, expressing his delight with the alterations made and assuring Anthea that they would be carried out without any problem. But her pleasure in thwarting Claudine was dispelled by the sight of her that evening.

Mark had decided to give a party to introduce his fiancée to his friends, explaining that it was expected of him and that Claudine and Jasper would be among the guests. Typically, they were the first to arrive.

Jasper caught hold of Anthea's hand and chuckled at her in a way that made her long to slap his face. 'I feel as if I engineered the whole thing. I'm sure my seeing you together spurred Mark into making a decision.'

'How unchivalrous of you to say so,' she replied coolly, and was pleased to see him look discomfited. But not so Claudine, who was very much in control of herself and said all the right things, exclaiming with pleasure over the engagement ring. But momentarily alone with Anthea later that evening, when coffee was being served, she was not so polite.

'I hope you aren't making the mistake of thinking you're a permanent fixture here? There won't be any need for your engagement to continue once I leave Jasper.'

'Then you'd better be quick about it,' Anthea answered, 'or I might start pressing Mark for a quick marriage.'

'He'd never agree.'

'He might not have any choice. If I threatened to tell the truth, it would make a marvellous story. The way you ran out of the house to escape your husband, and how I stepped in to save your reputation!'

Claudine's skin went mottled with temper. 'What about *your* reputation? Don't forget Jasper found you with Mark in the early hours of the morning. People might wonder if *your* story was true!'

'It might be worth losing my good name in order to tell the truth about yours.'

'You wouldn't dare!'

'Don't try me too far or I will.'

The rouge on Claudine's cheeks stood out in bright dabs of colour, making her look like the Doll in *Petrushka*. But she had the intelligence to know she had lost the argument and, with a shrug to signify it was unimportant, she moved away.

Resolutely Anthea remembered her duties as a hostess and moved from group to group, deliberately keeping away from Claudine and Jasper. It was nearly dawn before the party broke up, but as Anthea went towards the lift, Mark put his hand on her arm and stopped her.

'You did very well tonight. I've never seen Sir Roger Marrick so amused. What were you talking to him about?'

'The way I infiltrated into your life. He was laughing at the way I turned myself into a frump.'

Mark looked irritated and then wry. 'Laughing at my expense, eh?'

'I thought it best to turn the whole housekeeping episode into a joke. People will be less likely to remember it if they don't see it as some spicy sort of scandal.'

Mark immediately conceded the point. 'You're right, my dear. My apologies for not realising it myself.' He hesitated, then said: 'Why don't you go and see your parents in Portugal? I'm sure they would like to hear about our romance at first hand.'

'I would rather not lie to them, if you don't mind.'

'Tell them the truth. But I still want you to go away in a week's time.'

'Why?'

'You know I won't tell you,' he smiled. 'Just do as I ask and get out of the country.'

She struggled with the ring on her finger. 'There's no point going on with this pretence any longer.'

'Please,' he said, and put his hand over hers. Anthea could feel his fingers trembling. 'I have my reasons. For

175

heavens sake, don't argue with me. Pack a bag and go. We'll talk about breaking our engagement when you come back. It won't matter by then anyway.'

'What do you mean?'

'I'll book a ticket for you to Lisbon,' was his only reply. 'I'm sorry to spring it on you like this, but. . . .'

He walked away from her and, puzzled at his demand, she went upstairs. Though she longed to disobey him, or at least to question him further, there had been something in his manner that told her she would get nothing out of him until he was ready to disclose it. He had made a request, and he expected her to obey it. If she were really his fiancée, if he truly loved her, she might have had the right to insist on knowing what was going on. But she meant nothing to him except a cover for an ugly truth. If he asked her to go away, she had no choice but to do as he wished.

CHAPTER FOURTEEN

AT six o'clock in the afternoon of the next day, Anthea was being hugged by her father at Lisbon airport. The urge to burst into tears and tell him the true story of her engagement was so strong that only Maude's garrulously happy congratulations prevented her from doing so.

Her father had rented a small villa outside Estoril which, though less picturesque than Algarve, had the benefit of being considerably nearer Lisbon. Anthea was given a bedroom facing the sea, whose great Atlantic rollers crashed noisily on to the beach some hundred yards from her window.

'You'll find the water too cold for swimming in,' her father said as she came out to join him on the balcony that led from the living-room.

'In June?' Anthea commented, surprised.

'Even in August. According to the locals, the water never gets warm. Most of the tourists use a swimming pool.'

'I'll still give the sea a try. It's so much more refreshing.'

'You look as if you could do with a tone-up. Been gadding around since your engagement?'

'Not really. A few parties—nothing more.'

'It was all rather sudden, wasn't it?' Professor Wilmot remarked.

'I've been in love with him for a long time.' Anthea was glad she could at least be truthful on one point.

'I guessed you were. I felt there was something between you that day we came over to the manor.'

'Mark never loved me then.'

'I'm not sure about that,' her father continued. 'You looked a bit strange in that get-up you were going around in, but he was still extremely conscious of you as a person. He's a nice man, Anthea. If you can forget who he is, you should be very happy with him.'

'Forget who he is?'

'Forget his wealth, I mean. Don't let *who* he is make you forget *what* he is.'

Maude came out on to the balcony. 'A pity Mark didn't come with you,' she said. 'Too busy, I suppose. It must be difficult for him to get away from his commitments.' She chattered on about Mark, needing little encouragement beyond an occasional comment from her husband.

Anthea only half listened, her mind still busy with Mark's reasons for wanting her out of England. Again she was certain it had something to do with the two men who, in the past ten days, had been frequent visitors to the house. Mark often saw business people at home, but it was rare for him to do so continuously, and she suspected it stemmed from a desire for secrecy; that he did not wish anyone to know he was having discussions with a police inspector and

177

another official. Away from him, she was able to think more clearly, and she was convinced he wanted her absence in order to save her from something unpleasant.

The knowledge kept her on tenterhooks, and for the next few days she anxiously awaited a letter from him. None came and she chided herself for having expected one. After all, there was no reason for him to contact her, not even for the sake of pretence. But on the third day she was so restless that she almost put in a call to him, and was only prevented from doing so by the knowledge that in such a small villa any conversation she had with him would be overheard.

On the morning of the fourth day she was able to relax, and for the first time enjoyed the heat and the cooling breeze blowing in from the sea. It was still too early for many tourists, but there were sufficient people around to prevent the little town from being isolated, and she went for a stroll along the promenade and then took a detour back to the villa via the shops.

She had not read an English newspaper since she had left London, and passing a newsagent she went into see if she could buy one. There were none available and she was turning to walk out when she saw a picture of Mark and Jasper on the front page of a Portuguese paper. She bent to look at it, trying to make out the half-inch caption above it. But her knowledge of Portuguese was practically nil and she could make no sense of it.

'Please,' she asked the woman behind the counter, 'can you tell me what it says?'

The woman looked at her uncomprehendingly and Anthea picked up the paper and pointed to the photograph. Instantly she received a toothy smile and the paper was taken from her and carefully read.

'A beeg business has gone collapsed,' the woman said in fractured English. 'In—how you say—fraud scandal.' The head bent to the paper again. 'The police say he stand trial. It was discovered by—' the woman pursed her lips, having difficulty with the name—'by Jasper Goderick. He uncover truth. This one, he beeg crook.' A plump finger pointed at Mark's face. 'He crook and Senhor Goderick find out. Is terrible, no?'

Without replying Anthea fled. She had no conscious knowledge of returning to the villa, but she must have done so, for she found herself in her bedroom packing the case she had only unpacked a few days before. At last she knew why Mark had wanted her out of the country. At last she knew the reason for the police inspector's visits; for the long hours in the library and the strain on Mark's face. She knew too why Mark had been so anxious for Jasper not to learn he was in love with Claudine. Perhaps even as little as two weeks ago he had still hoped to avert disaster by merging with Jasper's company.

Somehow it all began to make horrifying sense. Mannerisms and phrases floated into her mind: Mark's tenseness; his irritability; his talk of building on shifting sand and of the dangers inherent in doing so. It was the knowledge that his business was crumbling that had no doubt prompted him to try and merge with Jasper Goderick. Had he been successful it would have saved him. But unfortunately he had not reckoned on Jasper's discovery of the truth. Could Jasper—jealous of Claudine's interest in Mark—have gone into Mark's affairs with more caution than he might otherwise have done? Whatever the reason, the truth had been discovered and Mark, knowing he could not avert disaster, had wanted her out of the way when the crash officially came.

Snapping her suitcase shut, she carried it down to the hall, and had set it on the floor when her father came in from the garden.

'I'm going back to London,' she said. 'Something has

happened to Mark.'

'Have you heard from him? Is he ill?'

'Not ill. It's to do with his business. I have to be with him.'

'What is it? You look like a ghost, Anthea. Would you like me to come back with you?'

Tears filled her eyes at the offer, but she shook her head. 'It's sweet of you to suggest it, darling, but I don't think Mark would want to see anyone. It's better if I go alone.'

'But you aren't booked on a plane.'

'I'll go to the airport and get on the first available flight. If you could arrange a taxi for me . . .?'

'I'll take you there myself.' He saw her expression and said: 'Don't worry, my dear. I won't pester you with questions. You've already made it clear you don't want to talk about it.'

This time her tears overflowed. 'You're more understanding than I deserve,' she cried, and flung herself into his arms.

'No more crying,' he said gruffly. 'All this dampness is bad for my rheumatism!'

She gave a shaky smile, and stepping out of his hold, wiped her eyes.

It was a quiet, composed Anthea who, some two hours later, boarded a Portuguese airliner bound for London.

'Telephone me as soon as you have any news,' her father said as she kissed him goodbye. 'And if you want to have me with you, just say the word and I'll fly home.'

She remembered his offer as the plane slowly taxied along the apron to its take-off position. Kind though it was, she could never avail herself of it; there would be too many explanations to give him—the truth about her engagement to Mark being the most difficult one of all.

The flight to London was a bumpy one but no more uncomfortable than her own thoughts, and she arrived nauseated and shaken at Heathrow. There had been no English papers on the aircraft, and once through Customs she made her way to the news-stand, intent on finding out the latest news.

A man knocked against her, apologising as he stepped back. He was holding a professional-looking camera, and glancing past him Anthea saw several other photographers in the vicinity. Hastily she hurried on, wondering if they could be looking out for her. Had they discovered she had gone to Portugal and was on her way back? Mark had continually told her that the newspapers hounded him, and she remembered his warning to her never to make any comments to them. Two more photographers came sidling in her direction, and she nervously backtracked. It was foolish to go to the news-stand. There might already be photographs of herself in the latest edition, and if someone recognised her from it.... Donning a pair of dark glasses, she picked up her suitcase and ran, only breathing a sigh of relief as she settled into the back of a hired car that had been waiting to pick up a fare outside the terminal building.

Unwilling to give the driver her real address, she told him merely to take her to the north side of Eaton Square, explaining that she lived down a mews and it was quicker for her to walk than involve him in a detour. He accepted this without comment, and three-quarters of an hour later deposited her at the intersection she had requested. Anthea paid him off and waited for him to drive away before heading towards the house. She was some fifteen yards away from it when she saw a group of men clustered at the bottom of the steps. Her first instinct was to turn tail and run, but afraid this might attract notice she set her teeth and walked on, keeping her eyes lowered as she came abreast of them and maintaining an even pace until she reached the next corner, when she broke into a run and headed for the mews which would bring her to the back entrance of the house. Desperately she hoped Dickson had left the door unbolted. She reached the garage and then came to the green wooden door that led into the patio, breathing a sigh of relief as it moved inwards at her touch. She stepped through and closed it behind her, then ran the few yards to the kitchen door. This was locked and she rang the bell, shaking with nerves and trying not to cry. The door opened and Monsieur Marcel stood there.

'Mademoiselle!' He was astonished. 'I thought you were in Portugal.'

'I came back to see Mr. Allen.'

'Grâce à Dieu! He will need you. It is always bad when a friend is involved.'

'Mr. Goderick was never a friend of Mr. Allen's,' she cried, and then stopped, knowing it was dangerous to say more.

'Maybe not a close friend,' the Frenchman said, 'but still close enough. And to do such a terrible thing. . . . There are so many people involved, mademoiselle. Thousands of investors have lost everything. Their entire savings!'

Anthea dropped her case and pushed past him, intent only on reaching Mark. In the main hall she stopped, not sure where he would be. She had gone through such turmoil in the last few hours that the tranquillity of the hall struck her as incongruous. A vase of flowers stood on the side table; a long Persian runner glowed like a dark jewel on the polished parquet floor and a dark green palm tree stood in a mahogany tub in one corner. Everything looked exactly the same as when she had left here; it was hard to believe that the world of its owner had come crashing down upon his head.

'Mark!' she called, and ran into the library. It was empty and she sped across to the drawing-room. This was empty too, and as she returned to the hall Dickson came out of the lift.

He was too well trained to show his surprise at the sight of her, and merely said: 'Mr. Allen is in his bedroom, if you are looking for him.'

Murmuring her thanks, Anthea raced up the stairs, too impatient to use the lift, and was breathless by the time she reached the second floor. Mark's room was at the far end and only as she came to it was she overcome by nerves. Before they could take a hold of her she rapped on the door and went in.

He was lying on the bed in a dressing gown, his face unshaven and flushed, though she was not sure if it was from excitement or tiredness. Speechlessly he stared at her, and she took advantage of his surprise and came boldly over to him.

'There didn't seem much point in staying in Portugal any longer. I thought I might . . . that I might be of more use to you here.'

'How? By trying to appease my conscience?' he asked bitterly. 'Do you have any idea how I feel? Of what I've gone through in the last couple of months?'

'I know it hasn't been easy for you. I wish you'd told me . . . given me the chance of helping you.'

'How?' he asked again. 'By telling me not to blame myself? By saying I did the only thing possible?'

'I don't know what I would have said,' she replied truthfully. 'I don't know enough about the circumstances to form an opinion.'

'That's never stopped you from judging me before! Are you sure you haven't come back to tell me what a swine I was to pretend friendship with a man and then put a knife in his back?' He half sat up. 'Or do you feel more sympathy for Claudine?'

'Don't!' Anthea cried. 'I've no pity for Claudine. Forget her.'

'I wish I could. Her behaviour sickened me.'

183

Anthea moistened her lips. So Claudine had already turned away from him. 'M-Mark,' she stammered, 'I'm so sorry. But surely you must have realised she wouldn't want you once you.... You can't have been so blind not to know the sort of woman she is?'

'I know exactly what she is.'

'But it didn't stop you. ...'

'No,' he said heavily, 'it didn't stop me from using her.'

It seemed a strange word, but she did not dwell on it, intent only on making him see that *she* was here instead to stand by him, to give him any help she could, no matter how paltry it was.

'Let *me* help you, Mark. I won't pretend I can forget the thousands of people who've lost their savings because of you—but I'm positive you didn't deliberately set out to swindle them. You were ambitious and you wanted to succeed too quickly. But you're not a crook—I'll never believe that—and even if they put you in prison, I'll still wait for you.'

'You'll *what*?' He jumped up from the bed, tall and menacing. The flush on his skin had deepened to red and his eyes—without their glasses—blazed at her. '*You will wait for me?*' he repeated.

She knew she had given herself away, but she did not care. If he could gain the smallest comfort from her love, it would be worth her loss of pride. 'Yes, Mark, I'll wait for you.'

'Until I come out of *prison*?'

'Yes.' She clasped her hands tightly. 'Do you think they will? I mean, if you sold everything you had, if you tried to pay back as much as you could? Or will they take everything anyway? I'm not sure what happens in a case like this,' she finished.

'You certainly aren't,' he said dryly, 'but you've obviously made up your mind I'll be left destitute.'

'What does it matter? You can begin again. We can even emigrate. You can make a new life for yourself in another country. The most important thing is not to give up.' She came close to him. 'I suppose you sent me away because you knew you were going to be discovered. But it was wrong of you. I *want* to be with you; to help you.'

'Why do you keep on about my being arrested?'

'I read it in the paper. At least, I didn't read it myself—the paper was Portuguese and the woman in the newsagent's translated it for me.'

'Translated it?' Mark echoed jerkily, and sank down on the bed. 'Please, Anthea, begin at the beginning and tell me how you found out about my downfall.'

'I saw a photograph of you and Jasper Goderick,' she said, and taking a deep breath, went on to tell him all she had learned. 'That's why I came back. I was sure Claudine wouldn't stand by you.' Her hands clenched. 'I could kill Jasper for what he did to you!'

'I think it's more on the cards that Jasper would like to kill me because of what I did to *him*.' There was an odd note in Mark's voice, a jubilance behind the weariness that made her look at him suspiciously. Was he becoming light-headed? Could it be a sign of shock? As though aware of what was going through her mind, he reached out and pulled her down beside him.

'Tell me again why you came back?' he said in a tight voice.

'To be with you. To let you know I'll ... I'll wait for you.'

'And if I'm left with nothing—what will you do then?'

'I'll get my degree and teach. I'm a good housekeeper too.'

'Perhaps I could become a butler when I come out of prison.'

'Don't joke!' she cried, and turning her face into his

185

shoulder burst into tears.

Mark put his arms around her and cradled her close, stroking her hair with a trembling hand. 'You fool,' he said tenderly. 'You silly little fool!'

'I know,' she gulped, 'but I can't help it. I know you don't love me, but I'll——'

'I do love you,' he interrupted. 'I love you so much that I've often felt like strangling you because you didn't know it.'

Her sobs stopped as if by magic, and she stared at him through tear-drenched eyes. 'You're making it up!'

'So you think me a liar as well as a crook?'

Her tears flowed again and he gave her a little shake. 'Anthea, don't,' he said fiercely. 'Don't you know when you're being teased?'

'How can you tease me at a time like this?'

'Because the time is right,' he said huskily. 'Here I was full of guilt and hating myself, then you walked in and made me feel it was good to be alive.'

'*I* did?'

'Of course you did! Wipe your eyes and listen to me. I don't know if the Portuguese papers got the story backwards or if your translator was standing on her head when she read it to you, but *Jasper* is the one who's been arrested for fraud, not me. *I* was the one who discovered it.'

'You?' she gasped.

'Yes. We were having merger talks, as you know, and I began to go through his books. He had kidded so many people for so long that I suppose he grew careless. Or maybe I was a bit more astute than the other people he'd been dealing with. Anyway, I realised what had been going on and I had to make a decision. Either to stop the talks and let him continue the way he was—building a bigger and bigger empire on fraud—or to take my information to the Director of Public Prosecutions.' He sighed. 'It wasn't an easy decision. I've know Jasper quite a few years and it goes against the grain to destroy someone, even though you despise what they're doing.'

Unbidden, Claudine came into her mind. Her expression must have given her away, for Mark gave her another shake. 'Claudine's known for years what Jasper was doing and she also knew it was only a matter of time before he was found out. So she offered to give me additional information about some of his deals.'

'Because she loved you?'

'Because she has a fair stake in Jasper's business. She pretended she was also against what he was doing, but I'm pretty sure she condoned it. Anyway, her evidence will save everyone a lot of time and effort. It will also add a few more years to Jasper's sentence, but that won't worry our Claudine.'

'So that's why she didn't want him to know she was seeing you?'

Mark nodded. 'Once the story broke, Jasper would realise it was because of me. She was afraid that if he knew she was seeing me he would also suspect *she'd* done the dirty on him.'

'As she did!'

'As she did,' he agreed. 'Once she knew Jasper's ship was sinking, she couldn't swim away from the wreck fast enough.'

For a brief moment Anthea paused. 'Is she swimming in your direction?'

Mark tried to look modest and failed. 'I believe that was her intention. However, I made it quite clear that I wasn't available.'

Anthea drew a deep breath. 'She as good as told me you were in love with each other.'

'She wanted you to think it. She felt if she could keep us apart she'd stand a better chance of getting me for herself.'

'She nearly succeeded. If I hadn't misunderstood the

story in the Portuguese papers, I'd never have come back.'

'You speak as if I've no mind of my own,' Mark protested.

'I'm not sure a man *has* against a determined woman.'

'Like you, you mean?'

'Like me,' she said, and pulled his head down to kiss him. 'When did you fall in love with me?'

'I'm not sure. I became aware of you when you started answering me back! Then when you put on that grey dress I bought you—and looked so ghastly in it—I felt such tenderness for you that I began to see what was happening. I knew for sure the day your parents came to tea and let the cat out of the bag.' His eyes twinkled. 'Or should I say let the girl out of the disguise?'

She giggled. 'You were so furious.'

'And jealous,' he added. 'You deliberately used Roger to annoy me.'

'You used Claudine.'

'I bet she didn't give you as many sleepless nights as Roger gave me!' He was unexpectedly savage. 'I'm going to make you pay for every one of them.'

'How?' she asked, nestling close.

'By making you spend the same number of sleepless hours with me.' He ran his lips along her cheek to her eyelids. 'That should cover us for our first month of marriage,' he said huskily.

'And after that?'

'I'll think of something. I'm nothing if not inventive!' Once more his mouth lay on hers, moving gently, insistently, with a promise of passion to come.

'Darling Mark,' she whispered. 'I always wanted to marry an inventor!'

Mills & Boon
Best Seller Romances

The very best of Mills & Boon Romances
brought back for those of you who missed
them when they were first published.
In April
we bring back the following four
great romantic titles.

THE GARDEN OF DREAMS
by Sara Craven

Lissa wasn't quite sure whether or not she really wanted to marry
the attractive Frenchman Paul de Gue, so she was glad to accept his
invitation to visit the family château and meet his relatives.
Unfortunately this also involved meeting the austere Comte Raoul de
Gue – who made it clear that he did *not* want Lissa marrying into
the family!

VALLEY OF THE VAPOURS
by Janet Dailey

If Tisha didn't get away from her domineering father soon, he and she
were going to come to blows! So she went off to spend a long holiday
with her sympathetic Aunt Blanche – and met Roarke Madison, who
was even fonder of telling her what to do than her father had been!

THE REBEL BRIDE
by Anne Hampson

Judy hadn't in the least wanted to marry Chris Voulis, but in the
time-honoured Cypriot way the marriage had been arranged for her.
'Start as you mean to go on', a more emancipated married friend had
advised her – and accordingly Judy had refused to be a real wife to
Chris until they knew each other better. She had won the first round
– but couldn't she still lose the game . . .?

THE BEACH OF SWEET RETURNS
by Margery Hilton

The little beach had been Kate's childhood paradise. But she returned
home to Malaya, a successful model, determined to make no
sentimental pilgrimages. For ever since her first unhappy love affair
Kate wore the cool assurance of her career as a defence she vowed no
man would ever break down. But she reckoned without
Brad Sheridan . . .

ROMANCE

Variety is the spice of romance

Each month, Mills & Boon publish new romances. New stories about people falling in love. A world of variety in romance – from the best writers in the romantic world. Choose from these titles in March.

STORMY VIGIL Elizabeth Graham
LAW OF THE JUNGLE Mary Wibberley
THE GOLDEN SPANIARD Rebecca Stratton
THE TRODDEN PATHS Jacqueline Gilbert
MAN OF TEAK Sue Peters
STAMP OF POSSESSION Sheila Strutt
LOVE'S DUEL Carole Mortimer
JUDITH Betty Neels
NOT FAR ENOUGH Margaret Pargeter
DISHONEST WOMAN Jessica Steele

On sale where you buy paperbacks. If you require further information or have any difficulty obtaining them, write to: Mills & Boon Reader Service, PO Box 236, Thornton Road, Croydon, Surrey CR9 3RU, England.

Mills & Boon
the rose of romance

Mills & Boon
Best Seller Romances

The very best of Mills & Boon
brought back for those of you
who missed reading them when they
were first published.
There are three other Best Seller Romances
for you to collect this month.

DARK HILLS RISING
by Anne Hampson

When Andrew MacNeill married Gail he made it clear that he did
not want a wife but a mother for his children; Gail, having thought
marriage was not for her since she had been badly scarred and
injured in an accident, told herself that all she wanted was to have
some children – any children – to mother. But was either of them
being completely honest?

HEART IN THE SUNLIGHT
by Lilian Peake

Norway, Noelle found when she went to work there, was a land of
sunlight, glorious scenery and charming people – with the exception,
unfortunately, of her boss, the infuriating Per Arneson!

DEAREST DEMON
by Violet Winspear

Destine felt that her life had ended when her young husband was
killed only hours after their wedding. In an effort to forget she took
a job in southern Spain – and met the man who, in all the world,
was the most likely to remind her of that tragedy she only wanted
to forget . . .

If you have difficulty in obtaining any of these books through
your local paperback retailer, write to:

Mills & Boon Reader Service
P.O. Box 236, Thornton Road, Croydon, Surrey, CR9 3RU